Jimgrim and a Secret Society

Jimgrim and a Secret Society

by Talbot Mundy

WILDSIDE PRESS

Published by
Wildside Press, LLC
www.wildsidepress.com

A *Secret Society* originally appeared
in the August 10th, 1922 issue
of *Adventure* magazine,
copyright © 1922 by Talbot Mundy.

CHAPTER I

"See here, Jim, you quit the British army!"

D' YOU remember Mark Twain's advice to read the Bible? It's good. There's one verse in particular in Genesis that quotes old Israel's dying words.

He says to his son Joseph —

"Deal kindly and truly with me; bury me not, I pray thee, in Egypt."

To my mind that sums up Egypt perfectly.

No sensible man can blame the Israelites for wanting to get away. It charms you for a while, but leaves you wondering why; and there's a sting in all of Egypt's favors just as surely as there's a scorpion or an adder underneath the first stone you turn, and a hidden trick in every bargain.

Like old Israel, I'd rather my carcass were disposed of almost anyhow than buried in Egypt's finest mausoleum. But it isn't bad fun all the same to sit on the big front veranda of Shepheard's Hotel in Cairo and watch the world go by. Sooner or later all trails cross at Cairo. It's a sort of adventurers' Clapham Junction.

James Schuyler Grim, Jeremy Ross, and Narayan Singh were with me in 1920, and Cairo was complaining bitterly that she hadn't a tourist to rob. All of us except Narayan Singh sat at a little table in the corner of Shepheard's Hotel veranda, with Jeremy bubbling jokes at intervals and none of us knowing what would happen next.

My friend Narayan Singh had borrowed a five-pound note from me and broken his rule of only getting drunk once in three months. His periodical debauch wasn't due for six or eight weeks — which was why I had dared to lend him money — but we had found his bedroom empty that morning of everything except an equally empty whisky bottle. He had even put the furniture out of the window, possessed by some distorted notion of getting even with the world for old wrongs, and we neither knew what had become of him, nor dared inquire.

He might be standing stark naked on top of the Pyramid, delivering a lecture on Swadeshi to the kites. Or he might be trying to invade a harem, proclaiming himself the deliverer of lost princesses. Basing conjecture solely on past occurrences, he was possibly at that minute storming the house of the High Commissioner, flourishing sheets of scribbled paper, wearing no trousers; and demanding to be washed in wine. He was certainly being bold, probably prayerful, and perhaps using scandalous language; but subject to those provisos there was no limit to what he might be doing.

The one sure thing was that we were his friends and would hear of it, if he should fall foul of the authorities. And the one best bet was not to call official attention to ourselves or him meanwhile. We weren't going to leave Narayan Singh in the lurch, for he was a man and a brother who had risked his neck with us; but we should have been idiots to go about asking for him at the moment. So we sat still and refused to worry, while Jeremy exploded jokes until he suddenly grew deadly serious and turned his fire on Grim.

"See here, Jim," he said, tossing his head to get the chestnut hair out of his eyes. "You quit the British Army!"

"Why?" demanded Grim, looking calmly at him, unastonished.

You never are astonished at anything Jeremy says or does, once you've known him for a few days.

"I'll tell you why. I know the British Army. They'll serve

you the same they served us Anzacs every time after a war was won — kick you and tell you to go to Hell. Got any money? No! Got a profession? No! Can you write signs — shear sheep — shave lumbermen — sell canned goods — cook for a fourpenny buster outfit? Those are the chaps who don't have to worry when the job slips out from under them. Can you splice wire rope, or ballyhoo the greenhorns outside a one-ring circus in a bush town? No! And you'll starve, when the British Army's through with you! There you sit, waiting for a red-necked swab with gold lace on his collar and the rim of a monocle eating the skin of his nose to tell you you're fired!"

Grim laughed.

"D'you think it's as bad as that, Jeremy?"

"It's worse! I've seen your sort — sacked from the army to cover a bad break made by some sore-bags in an armchair. They come to Australia in shoals. Sydney and Melbourne are lousy with them. Most of 'em would suicide if they weren't too proud to steal a gun. They end by joining the Salvation Army and calling with a can from house to house for swill and spud-peel! You grin — good lord! With that in front of you!"

"Don't you think I could land a job out here as interpreter or something?" Grim suggested pleasantly.

"You've a better chance of a contract to serve ice-cream in Hell! You one-track Yankee visionary! You're so dead set on cleaning up Arabia that you can't see daylight for the dust you've made. For the love of luck, think a minute. Will they fire you for knowing too much, and let you stay here in the country? Golly! I'll tell you exactly what's going to happen. The French Ambassador will tell the King of England to roll his hoop, and the Prince o' Wales will be sent to deputize. He'll apologize for your having saved the French from doing worse dirt than they did to Feisul; and Downing Street will be so bull-angry at having to know of your existence that they'll grease the cables and suspend all other business until you're cashiered in disgrace. You'll be kicked through your headstall, they'll be in such a hurry! It'll be: 'Out o' the country quick! No recommendation. No pension. Your back pay held up for a year in case of possible claims against you. Watch your step on the way out, and don't ever let us see your face again!' The U.S. consul will refuse to ship you to the States because you aren't a distressed seaman. The British won't ship you anywhere because you're not British. And in the end you'll have to do exactly what you might do now, if you'd listen to sense!"

"Sing on, Cassandra!" Grim laughed.

"Who the Hell's Cassandra?" demanded Jeremy.

"A lady in ancient Troy, who got out the *Evening News.*"

"Well, I'm no lady. Jim, you fire the British Empire before it fires you! Write out your resignation and file it, with compliments, before the French Ambassador has time to ring the front-door bell at Windsor Castle! If they ask you what for, tell 'em the War's over; maybe they don't know it!"

"I'd still be out of a job," Grim suggested.

"Join Ramsden and me. Grim, Ramsden, and Ross. Thirty-three and a third per cent. apiece of kicks as well as ha'pence. We'll take along Narayan Singh as office murderer. What do you say?"

Grim cocked one bushy eyebrow.

"I've got no money, so I can't buy into your firm, old scout. That's all about it."

Jeremy thrust out his jaw, and drummed his fingers on the table. "I've a draft for two thousand pounds in my pocket, and I don't know how much in the bank in Sydney. Haven't been home for five years and the bank may have busted, but I guess not. Rammy here's been saving two thirds of his income ever since pa died. Never mind what Rammy says at the moment, he'll put in two pounds to my one; take my word for it. We'll make you senior partner, Jim, 'cause you're the one who'll get the worst of it if we lose out, so you'll be cautious. Rammy can do the hard work; I'll think up ideas. I know millions of ways of making money."

That was the first I had heard of any such partnership, but I made no comment, for a man had come up the front steps whom I hadn't seen for years, but whom I have crossed two oceans more than once to have a talk with — a man of about my own size but twenty years older, upstanding and hale, without a gray hair on his head, although carrying rather more stomach than I would care to tote around. He saw me, smiled, and nodded, but turned to the left, choosing a table at the other end of the veranda, where he buried himself at once behind a newspaper.

"Wake up, Rammy!" said Jeremy, kicking my shin under the table. "Tell him you'll kill him if he don't come in with us! Tell him it's true that you've got capital. Go on!"

"It's true that I've saved something," I answered. "But a man's a fool who risks his savings. I'd like a partnership with you and Grim, if you've a prospect; but we ought to be able to work it without staking both capital and energy. There are lots of men with capital."

"Not in Egypt," said Jeremy. "All they'll buy here is manicure sets and big expensive cars. We're selling guts and gumption. We'd find ten Gyppies in five minutes to stake money for a crooked deal, but —"

"Suppose you argue a while with Grim," I answered. "I'll go talk with Meldrum Strange."

"Who the Hell's Meldrum?"

"One of the nine richest men in the world. I made a million for him once. Wherever Meldrum Strange is, something's doing. He's on the level, but a durned hard nut."

"Go crack him!" answered Jeremy. "I'll stay here and comb Jim out of the army like a louse out of a dog's hair. So long."

CHAPTER II

"We three now haven't a parasite between us."

I SAT DOWN beside Meldrum Strange without saying anything and it wasn't until the chair creaked under my weight that he laid the newspaper down.

"Oh, hello," he said then.

"Hello yourself," said I. "How's business?"

"I've gone out of business."

I looked hard at him and he at me. He was good to look at, with a face carved out of granite and a neat black beard. There was a suggestion of Ulysses Grant, with the same look of good humor balancing an iron will.

"I've come all the way from the States to see you," he said.

"Nothing else?"

"Just that," he answered, biting the end of a dark cigar.

"I don't believe you," I answered, "but I'll smoke while you elaborate the fiction."

"You're going out of business too," he said, passing me his leather case.

"I did that during the first year of the War," I answered. "Cleaned up in Abyssinia and quit for keeps."

"Uh. Who was behind that Abyssinian thing? You put it up to me. Cohn and Campbell fell, didn't they? Make anything?"

"Three times what they put in."

"Uh. What did you get?"

"Enough," I answered.

He nodded and began chewing his cigar.

"Well," he said presently, "I heard you were wandering in these parts. Tried to reach you by cable, but you'd left no address."

"Any banker out here would have delivered a message sooner or later," I answered, puzzled. I'm not used to being in such demand.

"I daresay. Nothing to keep me in Chicago. Came to look for you — P & O from Marseilles. Saw your name on the hotel register."

"Did you ask for me?"

"No. No hurry. Met some people. Up at Government House. Seems you've been trying your hand at international politics?"

"I've a friend who was interested. Helped him," I said.

"Did you like it?" he asked suddenly, looking sharply at me.

"You bet! We spiked a crooked game and pulled a good man out of a tight place."

"I'm in that game nowadays," he said.

He took hold of his chin in his left hand and eyed me steadily.

"Can you afford to be independent?"

I nodded.

"Got enough, eh? Good. Couldn't use a man who thought he needed money badly."

"What's eating you?" I asked. "The only time I handled your dollars you had me bonded."

"Couldn't get a bond to cover this. Need a man used to acting on his own responsibility, not given to talking — be depended on to keep important secrets — act coolly in emergency — knows the world in the widest sense — willing to have no other ambition than to unknot the international snarls. You'll fill the bill."

"You're wrong," I said. "My gifts are mechanical. You need a man with brains for a job like that. James Schuyler Grim is the man for you."

"Ah. Now let me see; they mentioned Grim — Major Grim, isn't he? American? Um-m-m. What do you know of him?"

"How d'you rate my opinion?"

"Ace-high, or I wouldn't have gone to this trouble to find you."

"I rate Grim ace-high plus, or I wouldn't have gone to Damascus with him on any such risky business," I answered.

"What else can you say for him?"

"The British Government thought highly enough of him to keep him in their Intelligence Department, while they were retrenching in every direction."

"Expects the sack now, does he?"

"Jeremy is trying to persuade him to resign."

"Who's Jeremy?"

"Jeremy Ross — Australian. Knows Arabic as well as Grim does. Kidnaped in the War and carried off into the heart of Arabia. Made good. Escaped — gathered a following — led them the whole length of Arabia — discovered a gold-mine — worked it — dollied out more than two thousand pounds — made himself a power in the land — and was finally rescued by Grim and me with the help of Narayan Singh and some Arabs. Made a present of his mine to Feisul the other day, as a private contribution to the Arab cause."

"Um-m-m. Mine any good?"

"Best I ever saw."

"Gave it to the Arabs, eh? Who's Narayan Singh?"

"Sikh. Friend of Grim's. Sepoy in the British Army. On a bat just now — discouraged."

"Broke?"

"Not while I've a nickel left."

"How long have you been acting banker to broken men?" Meldrum Strange demanded, looking at me curiously.

"Nothing to it," I answered. "But I'll back a good man when he's down the same way you helped the market in the 1907 panic. Maybe it'll pay me, same as buying stocks paid you. If it don't I'll take my loss, and you won't be any the wiser, Meldrum Strange."

"Extraordinary!" he said. "Most extraordinary! World full of coincidences. Time was I'd have doubted this. Looks too good."

"Same here," I said. "Few things fit without blacksmith-work and blasting. Study this right carefully before you submit proposals. We'd hate to let you down."

" 'We?' " he asked.

"All or none," I said. "When you showed up we were just beginning to talk partnership."

"Those your two friends opposite?"

He sat and looked at them for several minutes.

"The one with his back turned is Ross, I take it, and the other Grim?" he said at last. "You vouch for both of them, eh? I'm inclined to think you may be right."

He sat for five more minutes saying nothing, chewing steadily at the stump of his cigar, and every now and then casting a sidewise glance at me. At last he threw away the cigar with a gesture that meant he had made his mind up.

"Anyhow," he said, "men like you are scarce. It's like looking for a dime and finding a dollar bill. Bring 'em over here!"

I caught Grim's eye; and he and Jeremy strolled over, laughing at one of Jeremy's jokes. I introduced them and they sat down.

"You the old robber who cornered platinum?" asked Jeremy.

"In my youth I was guilty of that," Strange answered dryly.

"Hah! My old dad bought International Platinum stock at bottom on margin, and followed you all the way up! He invested the proceeds in a sheep station. My regards!" said Jeremy, with a wave of the hand that signified a lot of things. "You big whales all have barnacles on your belly. We three now haven't got a parasite between us."

"Isn't there a drunken Sikh?" Strange answered.

"There's a Sikh who happens to be drunk," said Jeremy.

"If you want to see some fun, old top, come with us. Grim can tell you. Grim's had to tidy up after him half-a-dozen times."

Grim volunteered no information. All he knew yet was that Meldrum Strange was a multimillionaire with a reputation for titanic thoroughness.

"Came to make Ramsden a business offer," said Strange abruptly. "He tells me you three are inseparable."

"Agreed five minutes ago," smiled Jeremy, with the air of a man raking in a jack-pot. "We're Grim, Ramsden, and Ross."

"What are you going to do?" asked Strange.

"Oh, anything. The world's full of things to do," said Jeremy. "What d'you want? We're charter members of the Jack-of-all-trades Union. Exploring expeditions fixed up while you wait. Kings dethroned and national boundaries rearranged to order. Mines discovered, opened up, and worked. Revolutions produced or prevented. Horses swapped. Teeth pulled by the piece or dozen. Everything contracted for, from flaying whales to raising potatoes on Mount Everest, wholesale jobs preferred. All you've got to do is name your requirements, write your check, and sign your contract on the dotted line. We do the rest. Shoot, old top; we're listening."

Strange glanced at me. He looked over at Grim, with no more result. Having agreed to be Jeremy's partners, there was nothing further for us to say in his behalf; and Strange saw the obvious logic of that after a minute.

"You didn't mention keeping secrets in your list of offerings," he said, holding out his cigar case.

Jeremy took one, balanced it on the end of one finger, tossed it, caught it between his teeth, apparently swallowed it whole, and handed the case back.

"Count 'em," was all he said.

There was the same number of cigars in the case as before, but one of them bore teeth-marks. Strange pulled it out, examined it, and tossed it with a laugh to Jeremy, who caught it, spun it point-downward on the table like a top, and while it still spun brought down the flat of his hand on it as if driving a nail into the wood. He removed his hand instantly, showing it empty. The cigar had disappeared, but a second later he produced it undamaged from his mouth with the other hand. It was superbly done, like all his tricks.

"Do you know how to do that?" he asked.

"No," said Strange.

"I know you don't. I've kept that secret twenty years. Show you another."

"No," Strange answered. "I get the drift of your genius. Major Grim, I understand you're senior partner of this unusual firm."

"We're ready to listen to your proposal," said Grim.

"Can I depend on your silence if you shouldn't like the offer after I've made it?"

"I've kept Government secrets for a number of years," Grim answered. "Depend on all three of us absolutely."

"Suppose you all come to my room."

"Here's the best place," Grim answered. "We can see all ways, and can't be overheard."

So, as happens I daresay oftener than folk suspect, a secret that had never yet passed the lips of its first guardian was trotted out, not within four walls, but in full view of the street.

"I'll begin at the beginning," said Strange, biting on a new cigar. "I'm an egoist. Nothing matters to a man but what he does. Not what he gets, but what he does. That's my religion, and the whole of it. I've amassed an enormous fortune. Never had partners. I regard my fortune as the product of my own use of natural gifts in compliance with universal laws. I never consciously broke a written law accumulating it, but I've often done things that experience has since taught me are not in the general interest, and I believe that what I do in the general interest is the only thing that counts as far as I'm concerned. I'm face to face with a fact, a question, and a condition. I have the fortune. What am I going to do with it? No good comes of doing things for people. That's the problem. What shall I do? It's up to me to use my money in the general interest."

"Why worry? Pay off a part of your national debt, and go to sleep," suggested Jeremy.

"Huh! I'd lie awake to curse myself if I wasted a nickel in that way," Strange retorted. "Our government would simply buy an extra battleship. If we all refused to pay for war there would be none. I've finished paying for it."

"Oh, are you one of those men without a country?" asked Jeremy blandly. "One red flag for all of us, and a world doing lockstep in time to the Internationale."

Strange liked that. The question threw light on Jeremy's own view-point. He laughed — just one gruff bark like a watchdog's.

"The man who doesn't put his country first might as well neglect his own body and expect to do business," he answered. "On the other hand, a state is composed of individuals, of whom I'm one, with an opinion. I obey the laws. There's not even wine in my cellar. But I make use of every opening the law allows to escape paying for armaments that I don't approve of. I lose income by it, because the tax-exempt securities come high; but that loss is part of my contribution to the general interest. That's what I, personally, do in that particular instance, and intend to keep on doing."

"Do you propose to start a society or hire us to preach?" Jeremy suggested.

"I belong to no societies. I'm an individualist, believing that what I do is my concern, and what other folk do is their concern, subject to the law as it stands on the statute books. Charity leaves me unconvinced. I don't care to endow colleges. I paid the men who taught me what I wanted to know, with money that I earned."

"Well? Where are we getting to?" demanded Grim.

"To this: I made my money all over the world. I propose to use it all over the world. Nobody can fool me with a bald statement that peoples are self-governing. They should be, but they're not given a chance to be. They're herded up in mobs, blarneyed, coaxed, cheated, and made fools of; and because some of them have free institutions, they're blamed for the result, while the real culprits get away with the plunder. I'm after the real culprits. I want you men to join me."

Grim whistled. So did Jeremy. So did I. Three notes of a rising scale.

"D'you suppose you've any right to take that on your-self?" asked Jeremy.

"As much right as any reformer has, and more," Strange answered, "for I intend to pay my own expenses! I'll make it my business to fall foul of these international crooks, who are laughing behind the scenes at the world's misery. My business is to seek those swine out, force an issue — a personal issue, mind — and swat them!"

"You want to be a sort of international police?" suggested Grim.

"I do not. An international police would be answerable to an international government, and there is none. These devils I'm after obey no government. Governments are tricked by them into furthering their designs. Governments are made up of individuals, each of whom can be worked, persuaded, bribed, blackmailed or deceived at some time in some way. The rascals I'm after play with kings and cabinets like pieces on a chess-board. They play crooked boss with the whole world for a stage, and they're safe because they've only got to deal with the representatives of majorities. They're persons, dealing with impersonal ministries. I'm going to make it a personal issue with them in every instance. But I have to work in secret, or I'll last about a minute and a half. That's how you three men happen to be the first who ever heard a word from me on a subject that I've been pondering for five-and-twenty years."

"Strange, old boy," said Jeremy. "You altruists are all plausible; and you all turn out in the end to be feathering your own nests."

"My impression of you is that you're honest," Strange answered.

"Honest? You don't know me," laughed Jeremy. "I posed as a prophet of Islam in an Arab village. They used to pay me to make the dead talk from their tombs, and I charged 'em so much extra for every ten years the corpse had been dead and buried. Sure I'm honest."

"You keep good company," Strange answered. "How about you, Ramsden? Are you interested?"

"Interested, yes," I answered. "Grim is the senior partner. Let's hear what he has to say."

"How about it, Major Grim?"

"How would it pay?" Grim asked.

"Five thousand dollars a year for each of you, and all expenses."

"Would you expect us to obey you blindly? The answer is 'No' in that case," Grim assured him.

"Strict confidence, and the best judgment of all of you. Once we agree together on a course my instructions must be carried out."

"How about additions to the staff? I'd have to choose the men I'll work with," said Grim.

"I approve of that."

"Very well, Mr. Strange. We three will talk it over and give you a definite answer tonight," said Grim; and we got up together and left Strange sitting there.

CHAPTER III

"I have sworn a vow. Henceforward I serve none but queens!"

WE HAD not yet made up our minds, but were dining with Meldrum Strange under a great ornamental palm by a splashing fountain, discussing anything from China to Peru that had no bearing on Strange's offer, when a coal-black Egyptian servant, arrayed in fez, silver-laced purple jacket, and white cotton smock, brought Grim a scented envelope. The scent had a peculiar, pervading strength that commanded attention without challenging. The envelope was made from linen, stiff, thick, and colored faintly mauve, but bore no address. The seal was of yellow wax, poured on liberally and bearing the impress of a man's thumb. No woman ever had a thumb of that size. Grim turned the thing over half a dozen times, the servant standing motionless behind his chair. When he tore it open at last the contents proved equally remarkable. In English, written with a damaged quill pen, was a message from Narayan Singh that looked as if he had held the paper in one unsteady hand at arm's length, and made stabs at it with the other. But it was to the point.

If the sahib will bring the other sahibs, he shall look into the eyes of heaven and know all about hell. The past is past. The future none knoweth. The present is now. Come at once.

NARAYAN SINGH.

Grim asked the servant for more particulars — his master's name, for instance, and where he lived. He answered in harsh Egyptian Arabic that he had been told to show us the way. He absolutely refused to say who had sent him, or whose paper the message was written on; and he denied all knowledge of Narayan Singh. All he professed to know was the way to the house where we were wanted immediately. So we all went upstairs and packed repeating pistols into the pockets of our tuxedos.

Meldrum Strange agreed to follow us in a hired auto, and to take careful bearings of whatever house we might enter; after which he would watch the place from a distance until midnight. If we didn't reappear by twelve o'clock, it was agreed that he should summon help and have the place raided.

Looking back, I rather wonder that we took so much precaution. Cairo was quiet. There hadn't been a political disturbance for six weeks, which is a long time as things go nowadays. The soldiers of the British garrison no longer had to go about in dozens for self-protection, and for more than a fortnight the rule against gathering in crowds had been suspended. Nevertheless, we were nervous, and kept that assignation armed.

A carriage waited for us in the luminous shadow in front of the hotel steps. It was a very sumptuous affair, drawn by two bay thoroughbreds and driven by another graven ebony image, in fez, blue frock-coat with silver buttons, and top-boots. There was a footman in similar livery, and behind the carriage, between the great C springs, was a platform for the enigma who had brought the message.

We were off at a clattering trot almost before the door slammed shut, swaying through the badly lighted streets to the tune of silver harness bells and the shouts of the driver and footman.

Mere pedestrians had to *"imshi"* and do it quick.

Lord! That was a carriage. We struck matches to admire the finery. It was lined with velvet, on which an artist had painted cupids and doves. There were solid silver brackets, holding silver tubes, that held real orchids — *cypropedium expensivum,* as Jeremy identified them.

The curtains that draped the windows were hand-made lace — Louis the Something-or-other — half as old as France; and the thing to put your feet on was covered with peacocks' bosoms done in wood, inlaid with semiprecious stones. There were mirrors galore to see your face in, but no way of seeing out of the windows without tearing the lace, and we didn't feel afraid enough to do that.

There was nothing to remind us of the ordinary, humdrum world, except the noisy exhaust of Meldrum Strange's hired car closely pursuing us, and even that sounded detached, you might say, like the sounds of next-door neighbors whom you don't yet know.

We didn't have to worry about what direction we were taking, since Strange was attending to that, but there seemed to be no effort made to confuse us. We kept to the straight, wide streets, and crossed an arm of the Nile by the stone bridge into the better residential quarter, where mansions stand amid palms and shrubbery behind high stone walls. Nor did we leave the Nile far behind us.

The faintly lighted interior of the carriage grew suddenly as dark as death as we passed under an echoing arch, and out again on gravel between an avenue of trees. We caught the click behind us of an iron gate, and wondered what Meldrum Strange would do, but hardly had time to think of him before the carriage came to a stand under a portico and the door was opened with a jerk.

We stepped out into a realm of mystery. We could see part of the outline of a great stone house, built in the semi-Oriental, barbaric style of modern Egypt; but the only light was from a Chinese paper lantern in the middle of the portico roof, throwing quivering golden shadows on a front door that was almost entirely covered with bronze Chinese dragons.

To right and left was a silhouette of fragrant shrubs against the blue Egyptian night; and there wasn't a sound except what we made. When the carriage drove away and the click of horseshoes vanished somewhere around a corner there was utter silence, until the man who had brought the message stepped up to the front door like a ghost and pushed an electric bell.

Did it ever strike you that sound has color? The din that bell made was dazzling, diamond white, reflecting all the colors of the prism in its facets. When I spoke of it afterwards I found that Grim had noticed the same thing.

It was about two minutes before the door opened. Two black six-footers, who looked smug enough to be eunuchs, swung both leaves of the door wide open suddenly, and stood aside with chins in the air to let us pass.

WE ENTERED a restfully lighted hall that might have belonged to a monastery, for it was all white stone without an ornament except simplicity. The ceiling was supported by plaster stone arches, and the whole effect was so unexpectedly different from that outside that it froze you into silence. It was like looking forward to the circus and finding yourself in church. There was even dim organ music descending from somewhere out of sight.

The stairs were on our right hand, of stone, severely plain, with a hand-forged iron balustrade that might have been plundered from an old New England mansion. The same black-visaged minion who had brought the note and rung the bell led the way up them, we following abreast, in step and silent until Jeremy whistled the first few bars of the "Dead March" from *Saul.*

"This feels like kissing a fish," he exclaimed. "There's no afterglow. Let's warm things up!"

But there was no need. We passed into yet another world before the echo of his words had died. I hardly mean that figuratively either. Through a high, warm gray-and-silver curtain at the stair-head we stepped into a nearly square, enormous room at the back of the house. Four, high-arched, open windows along one side overlooked the Nile.

Maybe you've seen the Nile through a window at night, with the curved spars of boats as old as Moses motionless against the purple sky and the moonlight bathing everything in silver silence? It's worth the trip.

The light within the room was of several colors, shining through stained-glass shades and causing all the rich furniture to glow in a sort of opalescent mystery. Simplicity was as much the key-note here as below; but this was simple extravagance. The carpet alone — one piece of old rose hand-work reaching from wall to wall — was likely worth the High Commissioner's year's salary; and the tapestry that covered the long wall facing the windows probably contributed to the fall of Marie Antoinette by helping bankrupt the poor devils who had to pay for it.

There was an Oriental touch, produced by long divans with silken cushions ranged against the walls. A door at the far end was hidden by a curtain of amber heads — old amber, each piece polished into ripeness on a woman's breast; I walked over and examined them.

We sat down facing the windows, sinking a foot deep into silken cushions — and sniffed; there was the same scent that was on the envelope — jasmine, I think, mixed with some subtler stuff — and still the same far-away chords of organ music.

"Let's sing hymns!" suggested Jeremy. "Or shall I do tricks? I know a dandy one with cushions."

"Please do both. I would love to watch you!" said a woman's voice; and though we hadn't heard the door move, we could see her behind the amber curtain. She came forward at once.

"Zelmira Poulakis," she announced, when we had told our names.

I may as well say right now, and have done with it, that I know nothing about women of her kind. My mother was a wrinkled old gray-haired lady with nothing subtle about her, but rather a plain straight-forwardness that made you understand; and somehow, she has always stood for Woman in my memory, most of the other types being incomprehensible — welcome to anything if they will let me alone in the smoking-room.

I suppose Zelmira Poulakis is a type, although I've never seen another like her. She is Levantine, and those she-

Levantines while they are still young are supple, vivacious, with eyes that say more than their lips, and lips that can kiss, curse or coax with equal genius. She had on a frock all stitched with glittering beetles' wings, that just a little more than reached her shins, and they were very shapely shins; it was charity and art to show them.

She had the poise and ease and grace that go with the sort of education women get, who are "presented" at the smaller European courts, and her jewels, which were few, were splendid, but hardly more so than her eyes.

Jeremy — you can't put him out of countenance — drew up a sort of throne made of elephants' tusks, and she sat down facing us, laughing, speaking English with only trace enough of accent to make it pretty.

"You look rather bewildered and I can't blame you," she began. "What must you have thought! But I've heard such wonderful accounts of you that I couldn't resist the temptation. Will you forgive me?"

"Not we!" laughed Jeremy. "Forgiveness would imply that we didn't like being here. If Narayan Singh is in your hands he's all right."

"But he isn't! Oh, he isn't! If only he were!" she exclaimed with a comical grimace.

"Suppose you shut up, Jeremy, and let her tell us," Grim suggested.

Well, she told us. She was good at telling things, and a beautiful woman in a gorgeous setting is hypnotic, mistrust her how you will. We three listened to the end without interrupting to challenge her statements.

"Last night," she began, "there was a ball at the Greek Legation. My husband was Greek, although I am not. I was returning from the ball in my carriage with a friend at about half-past four this morning, and had stopped at the door of my friend's house about a mile from here to set her down; in fact, she had already left the carriage and my footman was in the act of closing the carriage door, when he was suddenly thrust aside by an enormous Indian dressed in a turban and a blue serge suit. My footman is a giant, but the

Indian flung him aside with one hand with hardly an effort, and I'm afraid I screamed."

She appeared to be ashamed of having screamed, but Narayan Singh with two quarts of whisky inside him would frighten the Sphinx.

"My footman returned to the rescue very pluckily," she went on, "but the Indian threw him under the horses, which frightened them so badly that the coachman had all he could do to keep them from running away. My friend did run away. She has told me since that she ran indoors to get the servants, but by the time she had aroused them I was gone; so she went to bed, and hoped for the best. Philosophic, wasn't she?"

Grim was sitting on my right hand. He made no remark, and didn't change his facial expression; but I did notice a sudden stiffening of his muscles. You'll see exactly the same thing when an experienced hunter becomes aware of big game creeping out from cover.

"I don't know what the Indian intended in the first place." she continued, "but my scream apparently fired his imagination. He swore terribly in English — said that protecting queens in distress was his only occupation — and jumped into the carriage, shutting the door behind him with a slam that sounded like a big gun going off. That was too much for the horses altogether; they went off at a gallop. Luckily the footman had scrambled out from under their feet, and there is a foot-board behind the carriage; he caught hold of that and climbed on. The carriage went so fast that it was all he could do to hang on, although he tried to climb on the roof and come to my assistance that way; the top of the carriage is smooth and slippery, and the feat proved impossible.

"Really, it was the worst predicament! it was almost totally dark, but I could see the whites of the Indian's eyes, and his white teeth gleaming in the middle of his black beard, and I nearly fainted. But he sat down opposite me with his arms folded across his breast, and presently I grew calmer and began to think. You gentlemen, who are used to all sorts of wild adventures, would doubtless have known what to do; but I didn't.

"I even began to suspect my coachman and footman of being parties to a plot to carry me off somewhere; and the fact that the Indian did not try to molest me made it seem as if he might be acting on behalf of some one else. I found words at last and asked him in English what he wanted.

" 'Nothing under heaven but your Majesty's instructions!' he answered. 'I am Narayan Singh, your servant. Say but the word, your Majesty, and I will accomplish marvels — I will pull the heads off these Egyptians as a crow pulls worms out of a plowed field! Command me! Set me a task! My honor is involved! I have sworn a vow. Henceforward I serve none but queens!'

"Can you imagine it? I asked him to stop the horses! I couldn't think of anything else to tell him to do! I knew by the overpowering smell of whisky that he was intoxicated, but he seemed mad in the bargain. I wanted to get rid of him and I'm afraid the thought occurred to me that he might get killed in making the attempt, although I hardly hoped he would really try.

"However, he didn't hesitate for a second. The carriage was swaying all over the street, with the wheels grating against a curbstone one minute and skidding sidewise the next, and it was all I could do to keep my seat, to say nothing of standing up. But he opened the door, climbed out, swung himself up on the box beside the coachman, seized the reins, and tugged at them, discovered that was no use, and jumped on to the back of the near-side horse! Both horses nearly fell, and in the time they had recovered he had their heads together and was tugging them to a standstill! Strength — such strength — he nearly wrenched their heads off! And he brought them to a standstill beside a street lamp at a crossing, trembling and too thoroughly conquered to bolt again whatever happened!

"The footman jumped down then, and the Indian struck him, calling him names and ordering him to go and stand at the horses' heads. Then the Indian came to the window and asked what he should do next, and before I could think of anything to tell him to do he was back in the carriage with folded arms, shouting to the coachman to drive on.

"My servants didn't obey him at once, and he was going to get out and kill them, I think, so I called to them to drive straight home, thinking I might be able to get rid of the Indian at the gate. But not so. There is a servant who lives in the gate-house. He opened the gate as soon as he heard the carriage coming but before we entered I called out to the coachman to stop, which he did, with the horses' heads underneath the arch and the carriage outside. Then I thanked the Indian for having protected me and bade him good night. He bowed and got out; but instead of going away he climbed up behind on the foot-board and called to the coachman to drive on in.

"Nothing would make him get down again. He swore that he was my only protector, and that none should deprive him of the honor. He threatened to pull to pieces any one who sought to interfere, and used such frightful language, and made such a noise that I was afraid he would wake the whole neighborhood and cause a scandal.

"It occurred to me that I have an Indian in the house who might be able to manage him — a gentle old philosopher, who used to be my husband's friend, and whom I have allowed to live here since my husband died, because the house is so big, and he so quiet, and so dependent on charity in his old age, that it would have been hard-hearted not to. He is a wonderful old man. I have seen him calm human passions in a moment by his mere beneficence.

"So I made the best of an awkward situation by telling the coachman to drive on in. And Narayan Singh entered the house behind me, behaving like a family servitor except that he made more noise than ten ordinary men, and demanded to know which was my apartment, in order that he might lie down across the threshold and protect me. "Narendra Nath — that is the name of my old Indian friend — sleeps very little, spending most of the night on the floor above this one in meditation. I brought Narayan

Singh into this room, and sent for Narendra Nath, who seemed to appreciate the situation without my saying anything. He is a very wise old man, and never makes unnecessary fuss. He began talking to Narayan Singh in his own language, and within five minutes the two of them were on their way upstairs together, as friendly as you please.

"I retired. It was already after dawn, and I needed rest after all that excitement. But *déjeuner* was brought to me a little after midday, and after my toilet was made I sent for both Indians, hoping to get to the bottom of the affair and perhaps to glean some amusement from it. Believe me, I was more than amused; I was amazed.

"Narayan Singh, although not yet sober, had begun to return to his senses, and the two men had struck up a strong friendship. The surprising thing was not that Narayan Singh should worship Narendra Nath, for he is a venerable old man, but that Narendra Nath, who has so few friendships, should reciprocate. The two men had sworn to be inseparable, and old Narendra Nath implored me with tears in his eyes to take Narayan Singh into my service.

"How could I refuse? I would do almost anything to oblige Narendra Nath. But a difficulty arose at once, which seemed to admit of no solution. It seems that Narayan Singh is a deserter from the British Army and liable to arrest for that at any minute. What was to be done? I couldn't imagine.

"Narayan Singh spoke constantly of a certain Jimgrim and his two friends Ramsden and Jeremy — he spoke of you *tout court* — gave you no titles — and he vowed that you could accomplish anything — simply anything — between you. He spent about two hours telling me astonishing stories of your prowess, and it occurred to me at last that possibly you could get him out of the army in some way without his having to pay the penalty for desertion.

"But the problem then was how to reach you, and how to persuade you to take the necessary action, without letting the Indian's whereabouts be known. I thought of a hundred methods. I even considered calling on you at Shepheard's

Hotel, where he told me you were staying. But finally I hit on the solution of getting Narayan Singh to write a letter, and sending my carriage for you, hoping that perhaps curiosity would induce you where persuasion might have failed.

"However, the task of persuading remains, doesn't it! Can you arrange it, Major Grim, that Narayan Singh shall be discharged from the British Army, so that he may enter my service?"

Her smile as she asked that favor was the product of experience. She had tried it on a thousand different sorts of men, and used it now confidently. But Grim is a dry old rock, for all his vein of kindness.

"If I could see Narayan Singh himself, alone —" he suggested. And she found him harder to refuse than he did her, because his request was reasonable.

CHAPTER IV

*"Jaldee jaldee Secret Society Shaitan-log Eldums Range
Kabadar!"*

MADAME ZELMIRA POULAKIS did not argue the point,
but smiled exceedingly graciously and left the room by the
amber curtain route.

The beads hadn't ceased clicking behind her when
Jeremy started humming the words of one of those songs
that follow the British army eastward —

"Widows are *won*derful . . ."

You had to admit it. Wonderful she was. But no wise
fowler ever caught Grim yet by putting wonderful salt on
his tail. He was unconvinced, and looked it.

"Did you spot any flaws in her story?" he asked, and I
remembered that stiffening of the muscles I had noticed.

"To Hell with her story and your spots?" said Jeremy.
"She's perfect. Who cares if a woman draws a long bow?
Let's go odd man out to see who takes her to dinner tomor-
row eight. D'you want to bet me I don't pull it off?"

"Dine with her," Grim answered, "but explain this first:
Why did her friend not send servants for the police?"

"Scared stiff, of course," Jeremy retorted. "What Cairene
woman wouldn't be?"

"Well, her servants wouldn't be, for they hadn't seen the
Sikh. Why didn't they run for the police without her orders?
Did! she forbid them? If so, why?"

"How d'you know they didn't go for the police?" Jeremy objected.

"It's obvious. The police would have come here, questioned the servants, and taken Narayan Singh away. But there's another point; while the horses were running away they must have passed more than one policeman standing on duty. Why didn't the footman yell for help?"

"Too busy trying to climb on the carriage roof," Jeremy suggested.

"D'you believe that? You saw the footman. The carriage was the same we came in, for the paint was off the wheels where they hit the curb when the horses bolted. I'm no athlete, but I could climb from that rear platform to the roof. I don't care how fast the thing was going."

"Mm-mm, yes. But the footman's a Gyppy. He was scared," objected Jeremy. "She told a straight story. Straight enough anyhow. There's a gentleman friend somewhere, I suppose. You can't expect her to drag him in."

"Tell me, if you can, why the gateman here didn't call the police, when the carriage stopped under the arch and Narayan Singh refused to go away. Couldn't the gate-man, the coachman, and the footman have kept one Sikh outside the gate until the police came?"

"She didn't want to wake the neighbors," Jeremy remembered.

"Tut! Two more tuts! Half a hundred tuts!" Grim said. "You know Egypt as well as I do. There are only two things sacred in the whole country. Graft and privacy. You can commit any social crime in Egypt as long as you don't trespass around the ladies' quarters after dark. If she had summoned the neighbors, they'd have had their servants kill Narayan Singh. His body would have been tossed into the Nile and that would have been the end of the story. She knows that perfectly well. Now answer another question:

"Do you believe that drunk or sober Narayan Singh would desert from the Army, or pretend to desert, or imagine himself a deserter? He'd be much more likely to march up to

Government House and accuse the High Commissioner of treason! Listen!"

The music that seemed to come downward from the roof, and might reasonably be supposed to come from the upper story of the next house, suddenly pealed louder for a moment, and just as suddenly grew quiet, as if some one had opened the door of a music-room and closed it,

It may have been thirty seconds before the door closed again — if that was the secret of the burst of sound. It left all three of us feeling strangely disturbed. I have felt the same sensation when tigers prowled close to a tent at night. When the amber beads rattled even Jeremy gave a nervous start, although cool gall is his life blood.

But it was only Zelmira Poulakis back smiling and looking archly shy. I got the idea that she knew what Grim had been saying. An idea, according to Heine the German poet, is "any damned nonsense that comes into a man's head." However, you don't have to let people know everything that's in your thought; Grim made a pretty good bluff at looking cordial, I followed suit, and Jeremy is always cordial to a good-looking woman.

"I am going to ask you to come with me," she said.

She stood playing with the amber heads — stage-acting. She would have held breathless any audience that had paid for its seats; but you might say we were deadheads, a class that is notoriously super-critical.

And now, you fellows who are never afraid of women, laugh if you like. As I got off the divan I turned to hide the movement of my right hand, making sure that the automatic pistol wasn't caught in the pocket lining. The dead weight of it felt good. That's how much Zelmira Poulakis had me hypnotized.

Grim strode forward, and before he reached the curtain I whispered to Jeremy to keep behind me with both eyes lifting. He was humming a tune to himself, and his careless mood annoyed me.

I can't explain why I felt that way. Fear was ridiculous, as in the last analysis it always is; but I can close my eyes today and recall the sensation as vividly as if it had happened an hour ago.

She led us almost completely around the house through a series of magnificently furnished rooms with polished floors that must have needed an army of servants to keep them in shape. Some of the rooms had cut-glass electric chandeliers that blazed like clustered diamonds. And she walked through it all on high French heels as a goldfish swims in water — her natural habitat — she would have missed it if it weren't there, I daresay, but as it was, thought no more about the splendor than the air she breathed.

She led us at last up a rosewood stairway that had rose satin panels painted with Venuses and cupids, up two flights to a floor on which simplicity seemed all the rule again. There was a big, square landing done in plain white plaster, with an open stairway at each end and six oak doors on either side set deep in the wall.

And now we were in the midst of that infernal music. You could recognize it now. It was the stuff they play in Hindu temples when the entrance is barred to visitors and lord knows what strange rites are going on inside. It makes goose-flesh rise all over you — perfectly bloodsome stuff.

Zelmira Poulakis opened a door on the right without knocking and led the way into a room so blue with incense smoke that for a moment you could hardly breathe or see. There weren't any windows. Such light as there was came from about a dozen glowing colored lamps, and when your eyes got used to the smoke the place looked like the interior of a temple.

There was a high, gold-painted screen at one end, carved into the semblance of writhing snakes; and a huge wooden image of a god with more than his share of arms was set on a platform in the middle with its back up against the screen. The music was coming over the top of the screen, and through it, permeating the whole place, so that you seemed to breathe that beastly noise instead of air. There were a few rugs and cushions on the floor. And on our side of the screen the room had only two occupants besides ourselves.

Facing us as we entered, cross-legged on a small rug with his back toward the image of the god, sat Narayan Singh, scarcely recognizable. He was naked to the waist. The hair on his breast was glistening with a mixture of sweat and scented oil. His beard, which is usually curled and crisp, was straggling wild. And his long black hair, that he usually keeps tucked under a turban so neatly that you don't guess it's there, was knotted drunkenly to one side.

But his eyes were the worst of him. Half as large again as usual, as if he had been staring into the hell he promised we should know all about if we obeyed his summons. Yet they were hardly the eyes of a drunkard. At the first glance they looked terror-stricken, but the suggestion of fear vanished as you watched them. He seemed to be gazing out of this world into the next, and although Grim called him by name he took no notice whatever.

Facing Narayan Singh, cross-legged on a second rug, Narendra Nath sat meditating; and, as our hostess had assured us, he was venerable. Have you ever seen a man so advanced in years and free from care that he looks actually almost young again? That was Narendra Nath. He had a white beard falling nearly to his waist, thinner than a Westerner's beard would be, showing the line of his lean jaw. He was as bald as a bone, but had bushy eyebrows, underneath which shone luminous dark eyes.

The moment we entered he clapped a turban on his head, which made him look twenty years younger. To look from his eyes to his hands was like bridging a century in half a second. His hands were like a mummy's, but his eyes were a youth's, full of laughter and love — though love of what might be another problem.

Zelmira Poulakis and we three all greeted him, but he merely glanced once at us and said something in an undertone to Narayan Singh, who nodded almost imperceptibly. The Sikh seemed to be in a trance, and I suspected hasheesh on top of the whisky.

"You see, he is not really in a fit state to go away," said our hostess. "Narendra Nath will care for him, and under that kind influence he will soon recover. But the days will go by and the offense of desertion from the Army will increase. Now that you have seen him, can't you do something about it?"

Old Narendra Nath's bright orbs sought Grim's as if a great deal hung on the verdict, and for a space of several seconds I alone observed Narayan Singh. His eyes moved at last, closing in the process to their natural size. He studied each face swiftly, making sure he was unobserved, caught my eye, winked, smiled, nodded, and resumed his former mask of semi-hypnotized immobility.

I didn't hear what Grim said in answer to Zelmira Poulakis. Sure now that the Sikh was neither totally drunk nor drugged out of his senses — Sikhs can stand an enormous amount of both — I began edging toward the golden screen. But before I got close enough to see through its interstices, old Narendra Nath came thoroughly to life and jabbered in broken Arabic:

"Stop! Stop! Not there! Turn back! That is not for your eyes! Turn your head away!"

It was dark beyond the screen. I didn't get a chance to see through it. But the disturbance served my real purpose, for our hostess joined her protests to Narendra Nath's, and that gave me full excuse for facing about immediately in front of Narayan Singh with my heels on the mat that he squatted on.

"None of us ever interfere here," Madame Poulakis then explained. "It is understood that Narendra Nath has perfect privacy. We never spy on him in any way. Even my husband when he was living never looked behind that screen."

Her statement didn't seem quite to tally with her manner of entering the room without the formality of knocking. However, I wasn't disposed to quarrel with it. I stood with my thick legs together like a Prussian on parade and made apologies, while Narayan Singh tucked something carefully into my patent-leather shoe.

"Haven't we seen enough?" our hostess asked. "I know how terribly such an intrusion must have broken up

Narendra Nath's meditation. No such thing has happened since he came to live here, but it couldn't be helped for this once — could it? You forgive me, Narendra Nath?"

I guess old velvet-eyes knew English well enough. He bowed with the air of a philosopher too wise to bear resentment, but with just the added touch of authority required to suggest that he wasn't pleased, and Zelmira Poulakis marshaled us out of the room. The comparative silence in the plastered hall outside was like heaven after the grating, ghastly temple music, which again sounded more like organ notes now that the thick door shut it off.

Our hostess seemed in a hurry to get us away from that scene, but I paused long enough to stick a finger in my shoe. I found a folded piece of paper, and opened and read it as we followed downstairs and through room after room in Indian file.

In the middle of the first room I slipped it into Jeremy's hand from behind. He read it, laughed back over his shoulder at me, and passed it on to Grim, who read it in turn and crumpled it into his pocket. It was written on the same sort of note-paper as the message we received at the hotel, in the same unsteady hand, and with the same spread nib.

Jaldee jaldee Secret Society Shaitan-log Eldums Range Kabadar.

It wasn't hard to interpret superficially. *Jaldee* in Hindustanee means quick, or quickly. *Shaitan-log* means devil-folk. *Eldums Range* suggested Meldrum Strange, although there was room for doubt on that point, for so far as we were aware Narayan Singh had no knowledge of our millionaire friend. *Kabadar* means take care, or beware. Narayan Singh had evidently been interrupted before he could finish, for there was the beginning of another word — quite illegible — and the whole thing had been badly blotted by folding while the ink was wet. I took the message to mean:

"I must write in a hurry. There is a secret society whose members are bad people. Look out for Meldrum Strange."

True, it might have meant "beware of Meldrum Strange," but that was improbable. Joining secret societies wouldn't be in Strange's line, and his motives were indubitably honest.

When we reached that great reception room, and looked out on the Nile flowing lazily in moonlight with the secrets of fifty centuries safe-kept under its abundant mud, I didn't feel enamored of Meldrum Strange's business proposal. Felt more like leaving him to paddle his own canoe.

Let's get Narayan Singh out of this, thought I, *and beat it for a white man's country.*

But we were in her net already, and the lines were tightening.

We sat again on the divan with Zelmira Poulakis before us on the ivory throne affair.

"Can't you do anything for him?" she asked.

"I'm no longer in any way connected with the Army, and consequently I have no authority or influence," Grim answered.

She began humming to herself, drumming on the ivory with her finger-tips, and knitting her brows in deep thought. The frown made a dark shadow that suggested evil.

"Leave it to me," she said suddenly. "Please don't tell where he is. I must have time to consider. It was very kind of you to come. Now I'll ask your forgiveness again and order my carriage for you."

"I'll forgive you only on condition that you dine with us three tomorrow night!" Jeremy answered.

She laughed. No woman refuses Jeremy lightly.

"I couldn't come alone of course."

"Bring a friend. Bring two friends."

"Shepheard's? Do you know a Mr. Meldrum Strange who is staying there?"

"No," Grim answered before Jeremy could get a word in, and for about a second after that the frown on her forehead disappeared. She was palpably relieved to know that we didn't know Meldrum Strange.

"May I leave the answer to your invitation until the morning?" she asked. "I will send you a note."

Then she rang the bell and we talked pleasantries until the carriage came.

CHAPTER V

"The policy of the man in armor."

THERE was no sign of Meldrum Strange when we drove out of the great gate. Unable to see through the carriage windows, Jeremy and I opened both doors and leaned out to look for him until we reached the Nile bridge and there seemed no further use. All we learned by the maneuver was that nobody was riding on the rear platform, and I mentioned the fact to Grim, who had built a sort of fence of silence around himself. The men who make a practice of that can be counted on to spring surprises. He came out of his reverie the moment I spoke.

"Let's get out and walk home! Quick!" he said. "Don't stop the carriage."

Dress a man in blue box-cloth with silver buttons, put him up in full view of passers-by, and he'll look straight in front of him, either from pride or shame, whichever way he's constituted. Let him be used to getting down and opening the carriage door at a journey's end, and he'll behave as if it couldn't come open without his permission. Nobody heard. Nobody saw.

Jeremy, who jumped out last, closed the door after him, and we went and leaned over the bridge parapet, staring at the Nile, in full view of a policeman on point duty, who noticed nothing remarkable about the arrival from nowhere of three men in evening dress.

Excepting the Gyppy policeman we had the bridge all to ourselves.

There being three of us, we naturally had three opinions; and as Jeremy wasn't under the weather or anything like that, he naturally voiced his first, vaulting onto the parapet and sitting with his back to the moon.

"Black is black," he said emphatically. "That's why we insist on a white Australia. You can turn a white man yellow, but you can't make yellow white. Narayan Singh came mighty near to being white, but, you see, he's 'verted, That message is just drunken stuff. He's full of hashish. He's had a handsome offer of employment. He's fallen back at the same time under the influence of Hindu superstition. And he's just sufficiently sober to remember the Army and us, and to feel ashamed. So he sent for us and then invented that bunk about a secret society in order to excuse himself. The best thing we can do is to send an ambulance for him, and engage a smart lawyer to defend him at court martial on the ground of temporary insanity."

"Why wasn't Meldrum Strange waiting for us outside? He agreed to wait until midnight," was Grim's only comment at the moment.

"Let's go back and get Narayan Singh," I said. "He has chanced his arm along with us and never failed us. The drunker he is, and the more crazy in the head he is, the less excuse we've got for leaving him."

"Narayan Singh is neither drunk nor crazy," Grim said at last with an air of absolute finality. "One bottle of whisky makes him crazy, but the effect wears off in an hour or two. Did you notice his eyes? That's an old trick; lots of Indians can do it. He was sober enough to write two messages; sensible enough to slip the second into your shoe, and sane enough to have asked to be rescued if there were need of that. As for 'verting, he was never anything but a darned good Sikh and he never pretended, hoped, or wanted to be anything else. He has stumbled on the trail of something, and it's our job to follow up."

Jeremy laughed. Young countries like Australia produce

men who are young eternally. Unless accident overtakes him, Jeremy will probably be laughing at the world long after Grim and I have died of taking what we know too seriously.

"You're making 'roo-tail soup too early," he said. "Old man 'roo's not shot yet. All you've got is salt and water. See here; if that's a secret society how do they come to send for us, and why did she let us see all that temple stuff and learn where the Sikh is and all that? That isn't the way to keep secrets. Posh! The little widow, bless her, wants Narayan Singh. Probably some other rich woman in Cairo has a Sikh to wait on her, and our little friend is jealous. You can see through her make-up with half an eye. She's probably monkeying with five or six religions — takes up every new craze that comes along — believes in reading palms, astrology, Raja Yoga, Ouija, Spirit-raising, Black Magic, and flirting. You watch: Narayan Singh will be carrying love-letters before the week's out."

"It's obvious she wants Narayan Singh," Grim answered. "She needs him so badly that when he insisted on sending for us she had to give in to him. The perfectly good excuse about being a deserter is proof that he's in his right senses. He doesn't know I've resigned my commission, and thinks he can't be accused of desertion after reporting his whereabouts to me. No. There's a deep game on. Why did Zelmira Poulakis ask us whether we know Strange, and why wasn't he waiting outside for us as he promised?"

"Why did you tell her we didn't know him?" Jeremy retorted.

"For the same reason that you don't tell people how your tricks are done," Grim answered, looking at his watch. "It's time to go now. The carriage has reached the hotel. They'll look for us and drive away again. Let's get off the bridge and down a side street before they return this way."

So off we went arm-in-arm, Jeremy whistling truculently because he believed Grim's argument to be all nonsense, and Grim with his thinking cap on, indifferent to criticism. He never seems to worry about another man's opinion.

We had left the bridge and were down a side street when an auto in a hurry overtook us and Meldrum Strange called out to me.

"Jump in, all three of you, quick!" he exclaimed as the car slowed close to the curb, and almost before we had time to jump in the car was off again. It wasn't the same car that he had started out in that evening. He hardly resembled the same man. His urbanity had vanished and his lower lip protruded beyond the upper one pugnaciously. He sat with one elbow thrown back on the folded hood and his right fist clenched on his thigh. Somebody was going to catch it, head, heels, and bank account; no question about that.

"You men sleepy?" he snapped. "Bed? No? Go on, go on!" he barked at the chauffeur. "Drive faster!"

"Going to show us the red light district?" wondered Jeremy. "I'm surprised at a man of your standing! What would the minister say?"

"Red ruin!" Strange exploded. "Somebody shall pay for this night's work! Are you open to consider the offer I made you this morning? Don't answer me! Don't answer me! Wait till you've heard details. I won't take 'No' for answer till you've heard the facts!"

"Fire away, old top!" said Jeremy pleasantly. "We've been seeing things too — luxury — Oh, Lord! — heaven on one floor with Venus presiding — hell above it and the devil making music through thick smoke! Hell on top of heaven, think of that! Talk to me; the other two are crazy!"

"I'll not talk for this chauffeur," Strange snapped. "Wait till we — where's a good place? Tell the fellow where to go to."

"Gizeh!" Grim ordered, and we swung off westward in the direction of the Great Pyramid, where one of Egypt's few good motor roads runs straight as a die between overarching trees.

It was as lonely and silent a road as you could find in the universe. The trees on either hand loomed up like nothing earthly, against a purple sky powdered with stars, and a cool breeze, laden with the stench of Egypt, dried up the sweat on our foreheads. Flat lands, and irrigated fields criss-crossed by motionless shadow spread themselves in a scene that would have made an angel melancholy — until we sighted the Great Pyramid, and were glad we had come.

It looms up on your left above the trees some time before you get to it, and is so enormous that your senses refuse to adjust themselves to its proportions; for you've nothing else that you ever saw to compare it to, and the comparisons they give you in the guide books have no meaning. Men built it; that's the amazing thing — built it three thousand years before the Christian era, using blocks of stone that weigh eight hundred tons apiece. They not only jacked them into place, but fitted them so skillfully that after fifty centuries of constant movement of the earth's crust, with earthquakes thrown in at intervals, you still can't shove a knife-blade in between the joints. Go and try, if you don't believe me.

Its purpose surely is to flatten the conceit of any one who thinks himself a marvel-maker — architect, artist, engineer, politician, financier, labor-leader, or whatever he may be. It fills the bill, and Lord, it makes modern Egypt look a mean, unmanly place.

We left the car by the Mena House gate, with the chauffeur fast asleep in it the moment we turned our backs on him, and walked the rest of the way, none of us saying a word until we came out on top of a new-made government road beside a newly opened tomb, and could see the vast pile dwarfing the two monsters that stand in line with it. Then Jeremy said *"imshi"* suddenly, and we came to our senses — awake again in modern Egypt with its professional pests.

You wouldn't think a jackal could approach unseen across that moonlit level ground that hides the pyramid's foundations. You wouldn't think, for the silence, that a creature stirred, and least of all that any one would come and beg in that magnificent loneliness. But a hooded Arab had seen us and crept out of a tomb or somewhere to offer his services as guide, and the hale, well-fed ruffian whined as if God had forgotten him.

Nor would he go away. He spoke English, and insisted on his right to act as guide to any stranger coming there. Jeremy kicked him, at which he showed fight — a distinct relief after the whimpering. Then Meldrum Strange unwisely gave him money, and he went to call his friends, who came in a troop, all tugging at our sleeves and demanding backsheesh for nothing whatever.

Finally I made a bargain with the whole tribe. We would pay the market price for being guided through the pyramid passages, but wouldn't go in. Instead, we would sit down outside for as long as suited us, and they should keep watch at a decent distance, making sure that we didn't run off with the pyramid, and protecting us from interruption at the same time.

That being something for practically nothing, they agreed. We sat down on the lowest course of Gizeh's uncovered base, watched from fifty yards away by a row of hooded ghouls, who quarreled in whispers over how much more tribute they might have made us pay.

"Perhaps I was hardly fair with you fellows this morning," Strange began. "It's not my habit to discuss private affairs with any one. Perhaps I gave the impression of inviting you to join me in a hunt that hadn't started yet. If so it was a false impression.

"There is nothing new in this affair. The scene has only shifted from Chicago and New York to Cairo. I've been following this up since long before the War. During the War our Government engaged my services at a dollar a year, and I was forced to let this slide; but directly after the armistice was signed I took it up again."

"Thought you didn't approve of war?" Jeremy interrupted.

"I don't. But the War was a fact, and I tried to help win it, Some time prior to the War I became interested in shipping — not in a big way — there were four ships of fourteen thousand tons or so that I had to take over if I didn't want to lose all my investment. They were British ships, at that time in the harbor of Alexandria, without cargoes, and not particularly marketable. I planned to transfer them to the U.S. flag, without having much notion at the time what all that involved, and I sent a representative to Egypt to see if he couldn't drum up a cargo for the States that would pay expenses over.

"There was lots of cotton being shipped from Egypt to the States — millions of dollars' worth. My man made a bid to carry some of it, and ran foul of a contract between the Egyptian Board of Commerce and a British steamship line, that gave the British a monopoly of that traffic. The ships weren't transferred yet to the U.S. flag, you understand, but there was one British company that had all the business.

"My man stormed around, but got nowhere. I cabled him at last to get any old cargo that would do for ballast, and to bring the ships over. He met a merchant named Poulakis, who agreed to charter the ships. Have you any idea how tricky a thing is a charter party? That man Poulakis either bribed my agent or blackmailed him — I never could discover which; some men corrupt others automatically. My agent signed an agreement that had more flaws in it than you'd think possible to crowd on to one sheet of paper. I couldn't countermand it; my man had full authority, and our consul in Alexandria registered the contract. Damn it! I can see Poulakis smiling now!"

"Poulakis?" said Grim. "Was he married?"

"You bet he was married. Prettiest woman you ever set eyes on; but let me tell you first what happened to those ships. You never saw such a contract. It was stipulated Poulakis was to have unrestricted use of them at a ridiculously low figure for two voyages from Alexandria to New York or Boston, and for six months in any case. D'you get that? Six months. Money paid down in advance to bind the contract, and our consul's seal and signature on the document. Everything absolutely legal, and binding me hand and foot. Yet the name of Poulakis didn't appear. At the last minute he rang in a corporation in which he held shares.

"He had no trouble in getting cotton cargoes for all four ships. I daresay he could only get away with it once, but once was all he needed. He cut rates and loaded the ships full. Sent 'em to Boston. Loaded up a return cargo of Springfield rifles, ammunition, dynamite, bayonets, some quick-firing guns, revolvers, and lord knows what else — all down on the manifest as hardware. Ordered the ships to sea, and tried to run those cargoes into Egypt for some damned revolution or other!

"Maybe you don't know the law. I wasn't as familiar with it then as I am now! Those ships of mine were still under the British flag, you understand. Well, Poulakis spent no money on repairs or overhaul; one ship put into Gibraltar with her condensers out of kilter, and it took a week to fix 'em, but it didn't take the British a tenth of that time to learn what was under her hatches. They let her proceed on her voyage, but as each ship drew near the Egyptian coast, bum-boats came out at night to run the contraband. British caught 'em red-handed of course. British flag; British law; inside the three-mile limit. Confiscated everything, ships included.

"If I'd already transferred 'em to the U.S. flag, I might have been able to protect my investment. I don't know. As it was, all I could do was to fire the fool who had got me into the infernal mess, and try to get Poulakis into jail in order to clear my own character. I sent a trustworthy man to Egypt with orders to hire the best lawyer in the country and dig to the roots of the whole business. You'd think that should be easy, wouldn't you? Nothing more difficult.

"D'you know what the courts are like here? Each foreign consul has jurisdiction over his own nationals. Poulakis claimed he was a Greek, and set up a cast-iron alibi of being an innocent shareholder in the corporation that chartered the ships. The corporation was bankrupt and the directors had all bolted abroad.

"On top of that the British had their hands full of local

politics and didn't want the abortive revolution advertised. The lawyer we'd hired was an Englishman, and I daresay honest, but English first, as am I all the time. I don't blame him. From his point of view I was an American providing ships for gun-runners and trying to fix the blame on some one else. Besides, I wasn't on the spot; busy with another lawsuit in the States that might have cost me a couple of million if I'd neglected it.

"Nevertheless, it seemed to me that something should be done about Poulakis. It's a public duty to jump on a brute like that, and I owed it to myself to clear my name. So I saw the British Embassy in Washington and — you know how they are — made friends with them. Kind of politeness that reminds you of the way they finish the bearings of their machinery — but nothing doing — no ships back — only a friendly offer to soak Poulakis if that could be done without international complications. And mind you, they're men of their word.

"They must have got after Poulakis promptly; for the next thing Poulakis himself arrived in New York with a brand new wife, damned good looking woman she was, and she contrived to meet me at the house of a friend.

"I couldn't help be interested. She was wearing diamonds paid for from the profit made out of my ships, and that gave me a parental interest, you might say. Amused me, too, to figure out what her game might be. She wasn't more than twenty-two or twenty-three. It was possible she'd blab out just the hint I needed to flatten her husband thoroughly. And a pretty woman is — well —damn."

"We've seen her too," said Jeremy. "Go on."

"What do you mean?"

"If you've seen her, you know very well what I mean! Finish your story and we'll tell you ours."

"Well, she was direct; I'll say that for her, She had the impudence of a modern college girl with the skill of an old campaigner. I don't dance. We sat out in a corner of my friends' conservatory, and she asked me point blank whether I'd had enough of defeat at her husband's hands,

I assured her I hadn't started on him yet, and she laughed."

" 'Isn't he clever?' she asked me.

" 'Damned smart,' said I.

" 'Then why not make a truce with him,' said she, 'and form a partnership, and have the benefit of all his brains?'

"When a thing like that is sprung on you, you're mighty clever if you have an adroit answer ready. To draw out more information I asked her what sort of partnership her husband had to offer.

" 'He doesn't offer,' she answered. 'He compels!'

"I naturally smiled at that, and she elaborated, 'Mr. Poulakis,' she said, 'never makes friends until after he has given a taste of his power. If I could tell you the whole story of his courtship, you would understand me thoroughly. He loved me, but he did not marry me until my parents as well as I were aware that he could ruin all of us if we opposed him, and now I love him all the more because I know his power. His is the policy of the man in armor. The weak ones, who yield too easily, he makes use of, never trusting them; from among the strong ones he picks his friends. He has given you a taste of his strength, and unlike other rich men I could name you have started to fight back. When you went to the British Embassy you caused him inconvenience. He inquired about you, and came to have a look at you, unknown to yourself. Then he made ready to destroy you; and now that he is quite ready he has sent me to tell you this — that you may choose between peace or war.'

"Imagine listening to that kind of talk from a twenty-three-year-old girl in a house on Fifth Avenue! I didn't know whether to laugh or get furious."

"Why didn't you kiss her and make her furious?" suggested Jeremy.

"That's precisely what I did!" Strange answered. "But I asked her first what peace between a man like Poulakis and me would mean.

" 'You would give guarantees,' she said, 'and join us.'

"I asked her what she meant by 'us,' and then she let the cat out of the bag.

" 'We're the most powerful secret organization in the world,' she answered. 'Much more powerful than the Camorra. We make use of others, and leave to them the sardines, as it were, that are too small for our big net. We are so secret that we haven't a name. Our existence is known and terribly feared by many governments, but none can identify us. Our affairs are conducted by individuals, but very few individuals know more than two or three other members, so none can betray us.'

" 'And what do you mean by guarantees?' I asked.

" 'You will find them profitable,' she answered. 'You will be given a chance to redeem your losses over that ship transaction, in course of which you will break the laws of the United States and two or three other countries. And you will receive protection just as long as you behave. If you were to misbehave, you would be exposed and go to jail. There wouldn't be much that you could tell, but if you should try to be indiscreet you would be killed; and all the newspapers would denounce the Black Hand or the Ku Klux Klan, or the Camorra, or some other society that has a name. And if you don't accept this opportunity, Mr. Meldrum Strange, you will be hammered and whipped and bullied and defeated at every turn until you change your mind; for my husband is one who never allows another human to refuse him. If you elect to give your answer now to me, you will save yourself trouble. Otherwise the taming of Meldrum Strange will begin tomorrow morning!'

" 'All right,' said I. 'I'll give you my answer. Tell Poulakis I've kissed his wife. I take it he'll know what that means!'

"The most remarkable thing about it was that she didn't resist — at least, not much. She wouldn't let me kiss her a second time.

" 'I like you,' she said. 'You're the kind of man it's fun to fight with! So it's war, is it? Well, take this.'

"She took a diamond ring off the third finger of her left

hand and gave it to me. 'Send or give that back to me whenever you admit you're beaten!' she said.

"That was the last word I've had with her from then until now, although she sent me her photograph by mail at the time of her husband's death, or shortly after it. He died in his bed like a Christian, and I'm told the funeral was attended by representatives of every foreign government that keeps a consulate in Egypt. Here's the ring."

Meldrum Strange pulled out his watch chain, and unfastened from its end a hoop ring set all around with diamonds. The stones weren't very big, but when he passed us the ring to examine and Jeremy struck a match they flashed splendidly; and they were set, with skill that is rare nowadays, in a briar branch carved from platinum. It wasn't a ring that could he easily mistaken for another one; there was probably not another like it in the world; and inside it the initials Z.P. were inlaid in yellow gold.

"The fight began next morning at nine o'clock sure enough," said Strange. "The office safe in which I kept my private ledger was broken open when I reached the office, and the ledger was missing with most of my secrets in it. A few securities that were in there hadn't been touched."

CHAPTER VI

"The more I'm defeated the harder I fight."

STRANGE paused to light a cigar, clasped the ring on the end of his chain again, and smoked in silence for several minutes. The only creatures moving were the bats flitting between us and the moonlight, and the only sound was the murmur of the Arabs' voices from a hundred yards away, still discussing ways and means of making us pay tribute. The shadow of the Sphinx looked like the pit that silence came from.

"You've no idea what the loss of that ledger meant to me," Strange went on. "It wasn't so much the difficulty of recalling intricate details of business known to few except myself. Whoever stole it had the inside facts of my positions. If I'd chanced to be overextended at the time I'd have met my Waterloo. I still was disposed to laugh at the notion of war waged on me by a secret society; but within two days I had to fight like the Old Guard to keep myself out of the receiver's hands,

"Every interest I owned was attacked simultaneously. I'd no sooner holstered up one angle than I was squeezed in another. Rumors began to be whispered in the street about my solvency. Bankers who had hitherto trusted me implicitly began to ask for detailed statements at awkward moments, and to call loans without any definite excuse.

"It was no use squealing. You can't go to the police with a

yarn like that. They'd laugh at you; and if I'd gone with it to bank directors they'd have shut down on my credit like a ton of bricks. There wasn't a thing to do but fight on the defensive against an invisible enemy; and as always happens, when you really take your coat off and show what you're made of, it left me stronger than I started. It forced me to concentrate on stability, building up real resources. I had a clean stable by the time I had won the first round.

"So when the War came the fall of prices on the Stock Exchange didn't mean much to me, except that bankers who had sent for me a few months before began coming around to talk with me instead. I had big sums on demand deposit — and the shoe was on the other foot. I made millions supporting the market, saved the bacon of men who'd have been tickled to death six months before to see me down and out.

"And I'd learned principally this — that governments are figureheads. Governments don't want war. Nations don't want it, when they think; but they're never given a chance to think. War is brought on by the rascals who profit by it. They work the game in a thousand ways, irritating first one nation and then the other. The men who do the actual irritating are mostly blind victims of an inner clique of devils, who make mischief for sheer delight in doing it.

"I'd been twenty-five years pondering over the why of things, and that sharp experience I had served to tear away the veil. When we got into the War our Government put me just where I wanted to be, for I'm a hard man to put anywhere else. I was attached to the Secret Intelligence Department. and you'd be amazed to know what trails and cross-trails came under my notice. Of course, the game was to win the War. I'd no time to follow up ninety percent of what came my way, but I learned what my business was going to be after the War.

"I made up my mind, in the same way that other men take up charity or education. I decided to go devil-hunting. That's the name I call it by. And I didn't see why I shouldn't start on this Poulakis gang first of all.

"So I went to the British Embassy again, and had a long talk. That was rather like pulling the plug before starting, but it couldn't be helped, for I had to establish understanding with men who might otherwise put insuperable obstacles in the way of my doing anything.

"I did the same thing at the French and Italian Embassies, with the result that I have *carte blanche* as far as they can give it to me. On the other hand, in every instance some one in the embassy reported the conversations I'd had, and there were three separate attempts made to murder me within the week. On top of that, I was sent for by our people and cautioned not to take law into my own hands.

"It would take too long to tell you now all the ramifications of what followed. I had to lie low for a while, and I occupied the time in rearranging my affairs, making investments that can't be shaken as long as the U.S. holds together, and quietly picking up a man here and another there who'd be the makings of a first-class team. Then this man Poulakis died. I was rather sorry. I'd hoped to lay him by the heels, and I supposed his death would mean the end of his organization. However, he hadn't been dead and buried thirty days when a man walked into my office as calm as you please and asked me for Mrs. Poulakis's diamond ring!

"He gave his name as Andrieff Alexis, and he said with a smile like a well-fed cat's that he supposed I understood on what terms he would accept the ring back. We had quite a chin together. He told me the name of every man I'd talked with at the different embassies; the name of every man I'd hired for my private team, together with some of their past history; and many details of the steps I'd already taken toward the task I have in view.

"He ended by offering to take me over, gang and all, and he promised me more power in the world than I'd ever dreamed of if I'd swallow my prejudices and come on in. He said incidentally that Poulakis had only been a minor agent of the society, which he assured me was stronger than ever but in need of some new genuine American blood.

"So I threw him out of the office. He had the impudence to

call the police, and I had to give bail for appearance in the magistrate's court; but when the case was called he didn't appear to prosecute. He'd gone. Left the country.

"Well, I sent one of my best men to Egypt — a fellow who knew French and Arabic — with orders to do nothing but mix with the people and investigate. He lasted two months. He sent me a letter every day reporting progress, and by the time his information was beginning to be worth while they'd got him, and all that he knew of me into the bargain. He married a Levantine woman, and he's in the jail in Alexandria this minute on account of some dirty work. The truth is they'd no further use for him, so put him out of the way.

"I sent out a second man, with three assistants. Strict orders to do nothing but investigate, and to report to me in code. Fortunately it's one of those codes that can be changed completely in ten seconds, for the Poulakis-Alexis people had possession of it in a week, and actually had the gall to write me a letter composed in it. It was a clever letter, and the joke was on me, I admit.

"So I cabled for those fellows to come home and this time I sent a woman — a rip-snorter — Angel Halliday — a she-devil if ever there was one, but true to her salt. She'd worked for newspapers, and for several years for a detective agency. Face like a frozen chorus girl, and a brain that was one perennial question mark. She lasted three months, and got drowned — by accident according to the coroner — in a boating party out at Ramleh. They tell me there's a dreadful undertow at that place. They said she got drunk and fell overboard, but I'll believe it when I see that stone Sphinx the worse for liquor.

"I don't know how you men are, but the more I'm defeated the harder I fight. Casting about for ways and means I thought of Ramsden and decided to come here and see whether he wouldn't lend a hand. I took every precaution: started West by train, and returned to New York by auto in the night — boarded the *Adriatic* secretly under an assumed name, and kept in my stateroom all the way to

Southampton. There, if you please, I was met by a gentleman who called himself Antonio Gambetta, who said he'd reserved a compartment for me on the London Express, and presented the compliments of Madame Zelmira Poulakis and Mr. Andrieff Alexis! Can you beat it?

"I had a powwow in the British Foreign Office in London next day. They gave me afternoon tea and a letter to the High Commissioner out here, requesting him to accord me facilities, whatever those mean.

"I saw the High Commissioner, and he's a dandy. He explained more Egyptian politics in an hour than I could have picked up in a year from other people. Told me with one of his dry, explosive laughs that if I'd uncover that gang I'm after he'd resign his job in my favor! Made no bones about their being too much for his people. Says they've undermined the whole police force and corrupted every politician who wasn't already rotting to pieces! He admitted quite frankly that even if martial law were re-imposed there'd be no chance of scotching any but the small fry.

"Nothing remarkable happened between that talk I had with you fellows this morning and dinner-time, except that I was conscious once or twice of being watched; and in the afternoon, when I went to call on the bank through which I propose to draw on New York for funds, the manager told me that 'business firms' had been making inquiries about me. He refused to name any one in particular; said the inquiries had come through regular business channels.

"Can you wonder that when that note came during dinner I was willing to follow you in the auto? It crossed my mind that the message was a trick to get you fellows away from me. When you drove off, and I followed, four men got into the car behind and followed me. They kept their distance, and when we reached that bridge they had disappeared for the time being. But when you fellows drove through the gate of that house and it shut behind you I made my man drive to a corner, where there was a street lamp, and told him to put up the top.

"It occurred to me I'd be invisible inside the car then, but the car itself would be standing in a flood of light so that nobody could approach unseen, and I could watch the house conveniently.

"Well, he put the top up — sulkily muttering to himself; and he'd just finished when the auto that I had thought was following dashed up from the opposite direction — must have driven around several blocks to take me by surprise. Did it too. I was caught napping.

"The four men jumped out and into my car, knocking my chauffeur aside. Two of them sat on the seat in front of me with pistols pointed at my head, one man drove the car, and the other sat beside him. They weren't native Egyptians; they were Cairene dudes with polished finger-nails, physically contemptible, and out of breath from excitement and the mere jumping from one car into the other. But they had business-like guns, and I sat still, and I didn't make any motion that would suggest I had a gun of my own.

"I'm not given to making a fuss. The other fellow's sure to say something if you keep still long enough. The dude who sat on my left had a long, inquisitive, triangular nose with a smart smile underneath it, and he couldn't keep silent to save his soul.

" 'Let us hope for your sake that you have the ring with you, Mr. Meldrum Strange — the ring of Madame Poulakis,' he said. 'We are working on the theory that you have decided to be sensible. We are willing to pretend to believe that you came to Egypt for the sole purpose of capitulating. We are generous enough to suppose that you accumulated all those nice liquid resources in America, and arranged with bankers here, in order to be able to contribute substantially to our funds. At the house to which we will escort you, you will find all facilities in readiness for writing instructions to your bank; we even have a gold pen for you with a diamond on the end to scratch your nose with.'

"Well, as soon as he said that, of course, I realized that the odds were in my favor. A dead man can't write checks; they wanted me alive and fit for business. The car wasn't going fast; the driver didn't seem to know his business very well, and they were running every corner they came to, with the idea, I suppose, of confusing my sense of direction; and as luck would have it we ran right into an accident. Two huge limousines with women in them had collided and were swung across the street. There were two Egyptian policemen, about eight extravagantly dressed females, two chauffeurs, and two footmen all arguing at the top of their lungs, and a crowd was collecting to watch the fun.

"The driver of my car tried to pass on the sidewalk, and he used the crowd as if they were weeds and he driving a mower. But a lamp-post stopped him, and I just opened the door and stepped out. I guess they'd have used their guns in that pinch, but you see the cops were sore with them for disobeying the order to stop. They'd come near hurting quite a bunch of people. Maybe the cops wanted a change of argument anyway. They had to put their guns out of sight in a hurry, and I was glad I hadn't exhibited mine.

"I cleared out, as you may suppose. Didn't run. No need to. Simply walked back in the direction we'd come from. Hadn't much notion where I was, but guessed I'd find my way to somewhere if I kept on walking. I had it in mind to ask for police headquarters and start a hue and cry for you fellows, but hadn't much faith in the police after that talk with the High Commissioner.

"Walked along weighing the pros and cons of it, keeping to the broadest streets and out of the shadows as much as possible.

"I can't have been far away from the house you fellows entered — I knew I was heading toward the Nile — when my four friends turned up again in the same car, overtaking me; and although there were two or three carriages in sight, and half a dozen pedestrians, they slowed down while three of them opened fire.

"They made poor shooting, Lord be praised. Broke a window and splintered a painted wooden gate, but missed me by yards. However, I made believe I was mortally hit. Spun round once, and fell, as I once saw a man do on Fourteenth Street New York when the gangsters were fighting outside

Sharkey's Bar. And same as he did, I got up as soon as their backs were turned.

"Nobody inquired whether I was hurt or not. The carriages hurried by. The people on foot ran for cover, and no one seemed to be home in the house with the broken window. Not a cop in sight. I walked on, cursing the authorities and everybody. My dress suit was in a beastly mess.

"However, I came on an auto that had just brought some one home, and the chauffeur had a whisk-broom. Made him brush me down, and hired him for the night at any price he asked. Then, as it wasn't yet midnight, I drove to a street corner near the end of the bridge and waited. Didn't have to wait long. Saw that unmistakable carriage go by with the doors open and two of you fellows rubbering — waited a while longer to find out whether you were being followed — came after you — saw you standing on the bridge — and there you are. Now tell me what happened to you, and after that whether you won't all three help me bring these swine to book."

We had told him about half of our experience, first Jeremy, then I taking up the tale, with Grim tossing in a word or two at intervals, when I noticed a disturbance among the Arabs who were watching us. Desert moonlight outlines everything sharply, yet conceals all details; at a fair distance you can see a man distinctly, but can't tell his face from the back of his head. However, it seemed to me that some of that gang of licensed freebooters had turned about and were looking the other way. At the end of a couple of minutes I was sure of it.

Jeremy bit off a word mid-way. All four of us froze motionless in answer to that eerie thrill that warns you of something that is going to happen in the dark. It was absurd to imagine danger out in that place, for those Arabs would be deprived of their perquisites if visitors should come to serious harm. Yet danger frequently is absurd. Absurdity makes it dangerous. You refuse to believe in it, and it gets you while you laugh.

But we were in no mood to feel safe anywhere that night.

If those pyramid custodians had suddenly attacked us none of us would have been surprised. But as a matter of fact it was their business alertness that saved our skins whole, and when it came to settling with them I never paid extravagant largess more willingly.

Their claim is, and they enforce it chiefly by grace of clamor and importunity, that no man may approach those pyramids without their escort and without paying them for the privilege. It's a sure thing nobody gets by them.

The hotel, near which we had left our car, was well beyond normal earshot, as well as out of sight, so we had heard no other car come to a stand there. However, a car had come. During the interval while our chauffeur was being interrogated, the Arabs sat still, with some of them facing toward us and the rest turned about on the alert for new arrivals. So that, although six men presently came creeping uphill, avoiding the white road, the Guardians of Gizeh spotted them as owls spot mice; only, unlike owls, they promptly made a noise about it, not swooping down on silent wing, but setting up a view-halloo as they leapt to their feet and ran to meet the intruders half-way.

Quite a number of them — four or five at any rate — continued to watch us, and even came closer, lest in the disturbance we should escape without paying our scot.

About twelve of then pounced on the newcomers, and the cat-and-dog-fight argument that followed was typical of Egypt — wonderful, colorful calm slit to tatters by foul cursing that sounds like smashing dishes!

I don't care how phlegmatic you are by temperament, you'll hate that voice of Egypt, cursed and cursing. It's the mother of bad tempers and the poisoner of judgment, and how the British have lived and ruled in the midst of it these fifty years passes understanding. Though I am told there are idiots who envy them and want to grab their heritage.

"Hell! Let's get out of this!" exclaimed Jeremy. "Tourists, I'll bet you, come to knock souvenirs off monuments! Rammy, you pay the holdup men. Jim, I'll give you and Strange a minute's start and race you to the car."

Instead, we laughed. Danger had announced itself, incongruous again. As if answering Jeremy's proposal for a race, the starting shot rang through the stillness and a nickel bullet clicked on the ancient stone behind us, neatly bisecting the distance between Meldrum Strange and me.

CHAPTER VII

"We're invading the United States this year, you know!"

YOU couldn't pick a worse place in which to attack four able-bodied men possessed of repeating pistols — provided they know the Great Pyramid intimately, as we did not. We'd all of us read about the thing, and seen pictures of it; I had even been inside it twenty years before, and had a rather hazy memory of the entrance passage. I knew it led upward at a sharp angle, after first starting downward, but forgot all about Al Mamoun's forced opening that leads into the ascending passage, enabling you to reach the so-called King's Chamber without first tackling the rather difficult descent.

The Mamoun opening was before us. In the dark I mistook it for the proper one, which is several courses higher up; and the others clambered up to it after me. Imagining ourselves well in the mouth of the only entrance, peering out like insects from ninety million cubic feet of granite and limestone, we laughed to another tune, minded to stay there until morning if necessary.

But again the unexpected happened. The pyramid Arabs decamped.

I suppose that having no firearms they preferred to watch the battle from a distance, and I'd be hard put to it to say why they should have risked being shot in order to prevent strangers of an alien race from shooting one another.

The Arabs had hardly vanished before the game, what-ever the game might he, was on in deadly earnest.

The enemy were not using pistols after the first few rounds. They had rifles fitted with Maxim silencers, and made damned straight shooting. Out of seven shots, for instance, they put three through Jeremy's tuxedo jacket; he was propping it on a stick and fooling them beautifully, but there aren't many men who could beat that shooting at three hundred yards by moonlight, especially when you consider we were fifty feet above ground level. These evi-dently weren't the dudes with polished finger-nails who had missed Strange in the street. They were gunmen.

Because of the silencers we couldn't tell for a long time how many men there were. They were behind some débris thrown out of a newly excavated tomb, but the **clip-clip** of bullets kept up so steadily all around us that we supposed at least six men were blazing away. It was Grim who spot-ted there were only three of them.

"I've been watching the flash. Three men shooting to keep us occupied. What are the other three up to?"

"Laying a blasting charge under the Pyramid!" suggested Jeremy. "Who cares what they're up to? I like to see 'em work!"

I had said we were safe in the only entrance, and we had all been intent on watching the shadow creep slowly sidewise as the moon pursued her destiny, inch by inch uncovering the ground our enemy had chosen. They lay at last distinctly visible — three men crouching on a heap of broken rock — three parallel dark blots. And there had cer-tainly been six men.

"I counted six," said Meldrum Strange. His voice sounded nervous.

"Six there surely were," said Grim. "If they're active men they may have climbed on the pyramid somewhere behind us. They could come along one of the upper courses and then jump on us from above."

"If that's all, we needn't worry," I answered. "Dropping down on top of us in face of their friends' fire would be a bit too dangerous for men who're not committing suicide. All we need do is retire farther into the hole whenever there's a pause in the shooting."

It was conjurer Jeremy who saved that night for us, and only in the nick of time.

"The hand deceives the eye," he said, and whistled. "There's a game on. We've watched three. The other three worked it. We didn't build this pyramid. Who said it's solid? Jim, you're skipper; shoot!"

"All right. Back into the hole!" Grim answered. "The light'll be in our favor if they try to rush the entrance."

Strange struck a match, but the draft blew it out. We entered in single file, Grim leading, all bending low because the bullets coming upward at an angle threatened nothing but our heads. It's no use trying to tell how dark it was. Each kept one hand on the shoulder of the man in front and we did a lockstep into the womb of dreadful night, pursued by bullets that clicked overhead and sent noises like the ticking of an enormous mechanism along into the dark ahead of us. Those sounds and their echoes were almost our undoing, for they prevented our hearing others that were less assertive and more deadly.

Mamoun's forced entrance that we were in isn't very long. We began to see ahead of us a patch of darkness less opaque. Whereas we might have been blind before, there was proof now that we had eyes; we could actually see the darkness, which was puzzling because the farther we advanced the less light there ought to have been. But we had forgotten about Mamoun's passage. It was Grim, groping the way in the lead, who first got the hang of things and realized that our passage was a false one, leading at an angle into the real.

"Something wrong," he said. "The stone's all rough."

His voice went booming away ahead of us until the echoes died in a gurgle somewhere. Then suddenly he shouted:

"Down everybody! Flat down!"

If our nerves hadn't been strung to the jumping point, that would have been our last experience in this world. But we went down like a set of ninepins all together, just as two pistols each flashed three times, and I swear I could feel the wind of a bullet breathe along my backbone as I fell prone alongside Jeremy.

I've never been able to believe those tales about taking in a whole situation by pistol-flash. I think they're usually what the French call *l'esprit d'escalier* — the things that occur to a man on the way down-stairs, that he might have thought of at the time if he'd had wit enough. The first and only instinct aroused by a pistol flash a few yards from my face is the necessity to fight like two men and a boy; and I'll answer for four men on that occasion — Grim, who has met as many emergencies as any fellow living; Strange, a millionaire, whose fighting had all been done hitherto in law-courts and on the Stock Exchange; Jeremy, self-trained for the love of it in the art of legerdemain, which means swift hand, swifter eye, and swiftest wit; and myself. Not one of us knew quite what had happened. Not one of us failed to fight back instantly.

Our antagonists came on before we had time to draw our own pistols. Having the advantage of surprise they made the most of it, and were on top of us before the after-flash had left our eyes. But they were on top of the wrong outfit for what you'd call a comfortable time, and three to four in the bargain, which is awkward odds.

I don't know what the others did. I got a man's leg in both hands, and a kick in the teeth from Grim's heel that didn't pacify me any to speak of; and I'd hate to have to go through life with what was left of the fellow's leg when I had finished with it. We weren't fighting in the dark any more, for they loosed their pistols off like fireworks; but a gunman is at a disadvantage at close range, for he puts faith in his weapon and is just that much handicapped. There's a little nick in my right ear that I came by that night, and Jeremy's cheek got hurried a bit; Grim's left hand was barked by a bullet; Strange got a kick in the stomach that took his wind and made him vomit, and a bullet through the skin under his lower left rib. Otherwise, although they had emptied their pistols before we really got going, those three men had nothing much to brag about.

So FAR so good. I dare say thirty seconds saw the end of them with my great rump planted firmly on the stomach of a man too stunned to squirm much, and Strange close beside me making noises like a sea-sick excursionist. Jeremy was holding down two men — the one whose leg I'd twisted and another, and Grim was already scouting forward to see whether by any chance the enemy had reserves in hiding around the corner in the other passage.

I guess we should have been caught again, and done for this time, if one of Jeremy's prisoners hadn't started screaming.

Funny, isn't it, how old memories crop up. The only man I ever had heard scream that way was a tramp, who was being washed against his will in a small-town lock-up; you could hear him all over town, and the women sent a committee of twenty to investigate. That was forty years ago, but the whole picture came to mind that instant; the tramp was given ham and eggs for supper and five dollars, which at the time impressed my schoolboy mind in a way no scream ever did.

Yet I don't believe I recalled the incident for thirty-five years until that fellow started screaming in the pyramid passage, and I knew he wasn't hurt but merely summoning the neighbors.

They came with rifles, in place of ham and eggs — three of them, scrambling up the rough stone blocks outside — and I heard them, thanks to that uncleanly but strategic tramp, whose shade may Allah bless!

"Out of this!" I shouted. "Straight on — up the ramp — into the King's Chamber — we can hold out up there till Christmas!"

Grim led the way with a hand on the wall; Jeremy pulled Strange along, half-supporting half-dragging him until his wind should recover; and having nothing else to do with one hand, I seized the fellow who was doing all the screaming and dragged him last.

I was possessed of a good notion and a bad one, although opinions may differ as to which was which.

I thought that a man who could feel so sorry for himself, if made a mite more sorry, could be induced to tell tales out of school. And it further seemed to me that, since he had been so keen to summon the riflemen, he might as well act as a shield between us and their bullets. He wasn't much of a shield, for he wriggled like an eel and didn't weigh more than a hundred and twenty pounds or so; moreover, he managed to draw an ordinary pocket-knife and tried to stab me with it, neglecting fortunately in his panic to open the blade. If I had let him have his way and break free he would have been shot dead by his friends, for we were hardly around the bend in the passage before the three riflemen stopped to fire a volley, and I guess they fired low by the way the bullets acted.

They surely were ruthless. It didn't matter to them whom they hit, provided they killed us in the bargain. The man I had been sitting on was shot, for I heard him yell, and the other fellow, whom Jeremy had been holding, roared out to them in French to hold their fire. They dropped him with the second volley. It didn't seem to me to be a good gang to belong to, and I wondered whether they had drawn lots, or what, for the privilege of taking us in the rear. Anyhow, I had saved the life of my enemy, so for once I was a Christian in deed if not by intention.

Have you ever seen a diagram of the inside of the Great Pyramid? The passages bear about the same proportion to the whole bulk that a worm-hole does to an apple. There's a long, low, straight, narrow passage leading upward at an angle of twenty-five degrees that opens into what is called the Grand Gallery, which leads upward again to the very center of the Pyramid and to what guide-books call the King's Chamber. The authorities had laid wooden boards on the narrow floor of the ascending passage with frets across to make the ascent easier for tourists; so, once Grim had groped for the lower end in the dark, we went up at a fair pace, Jeremy falling back behind me as soon as

Strange had his second wind, shooting his pistol off at random to delay pursuit.

There's a well-shaft, leading down into a cavern in the foundations at a break in the floor, and another passage leading into the small Queen's Chamber at the point where the ascending ramp opens into the Grand Gallery, and there we stopped to consider matters. Provided we kept back out of the line of fire we were safe there against anyone or anything unless they tried to smoke us out, which was almost an impossibility without cans of poison gas, for it would take hours and limitless fuel to produce smoke enough. Neither did running away any farther from three men, although they had rifles, seem to be the game.

"Let's go for them!" said Jeremy, who never recommended or enjoyed Fabian tactics in all his life.

The words were hardly out of his mouth when a fool at the bottom of the ramp switched on a flashlight, and the man beside him fired a shot at random. All four of us returned the shot. The flashlight fell, with the switch on, and across the pool of light it made we saw the legs of three men vanishing. I guess two of them were pretty badly hit, and Jeremy, who went down at once to get the flashlight, reported considerable blood on the stone at the foot of the ramp.

It looked rather like the end of hostilities for that night. It was dusty and hot inside that mountain of stone; we were all getting thirsty, especially Strange, and there was nothing amusing in the prospect of a vigil in there until dawn. But, as Grim remarked, we'd probably get sniped on our way out if we tried to escape before daylight.

"And besides, we've a prisoner."

Jeremy turned the flashlight on him. He started to yell again as if he were being tortured.

"You're making a noise too soon," said Grim. "We're going to question you, and if your statements don't tally with what we know, we're going to put the glowing ends of cigarettes to all the tender places we can find."

I disliked the prospect of that nearly as much as our prisoner did. When Grim says a thing he means it, and I would not have refused to help him.

The prisoner was a good-looking fellow, a little bit too smoothly groomed and rounded off to win instant favor with any but the underworld. His silk suit was torn, but he still looked foppish. One side of his face was almost intellectual, the other obviously criminal, and both sides were impudent, his bright eyes peering at you sharply like a sparrow's. There was a something pathetic about him that you couldn't exactly diagnose, and he had little bits of feet encased in patent-leather shoes, and jeweled rings on three fingers of each hand.

"We'll take you where your yells can't be heard," said Grim. "Where's the King's Chamber, Ramsden?"

You couldn't miss the way, now that we had a light — up the Grand Gallery, climbing along the ramp on one side — under a low block that they call the Granite Leaf — through a tiny antechamber — and into the Mystery of Mysteries, the oblong room with unadorned, polished granite walls, containing a stone-sarcophagus that never held mummy nor had lid. I've read eight or nine books that pretend to tell the secret of that thirty-four by seventeen room in the midst of ninety million cubic feet of squared stone and don't believe that any of them have it right. It's still the mother of all secrets — as the Sphinx, smiling outside in the desert admits — and the very place in which to hear secrets told. We sat our prisoner down on the dusty floor with his back to the sarcophagus, and Grim, squatting down in front of him, got busy.

Grim is an expert. He goes at his man as if unraveling a knot, picking out the key-snarl cannily. I would have asked what the fighting meant, beginning at the loose end, as it were, but not so he. He began by requesting us all to light cigarettes, so we leaned with our backs against the wall facing the entrance and smoked, although the sweat was streaming from us and tobacco tasted like salt fish; but the hint wasn't lost on our prisoner.

"You gentlemen wouldn't do such a thing as that?" he

whined in English. "You look like decent men, surely you wouldn't demean yourselves by burning a little man like me? You're not seriously injured, and it wasn't I who —"

"Answer me!" Grim commanded. "On what terms may Mr. Meldrum Strange surrender, and to whom?"

If he had turned and shot me, I wouldn't have been more astonished. The face of Meldrum Strange was good to see.

"Why — to Madame Poulakis — he must marry Madame Poulakis — that is understood. He must marry her and make settlement."

Strange coughed explosively, too contemptuous for words.

"Maybe I'd do instead?" Jeremy suggested. "I'd settle a rosy future on her. Strange, old boy, why not hire me to act substitute?"

"It's not too late to surrender?" demanded Grim.

Our prisoner answered excitedly:

"Why no; no, no; of course not! Our people would be quite satisfied — only we all have to commit ourselves, you know, or there'd be no loyalty."

"Your people, eh? What's your name? Quick! Out with it!"

"Oh, I don't mind telling you Poulakis is my name. I'm a nephew of the great Poulakis; everybody knows that. Ask any one in Cairo, and they'll tell I'm mixed up in all the Hig' Lif'. But you can't get evidence against me; that's where the rub comes in! I've been tried lots of times. I've even been court martialed. Hee!"

He was recovering his vanity, which is what some men pack instead of pluck. It's often hard to tell the difference, until you prick the container.

"Suppose we take off one of those silk socks and a pretty patent-leather shoe. They say there's a place between a man's toes where fire hurts horribly," said Grim.

Mr. Poulakis junior sat on both feet at once like a Turk and shuddered. Jeremy held the spotlight on him steadily and he hadn't a private emotion left — couldn't glance timidly sidewise at us without Grim knowing it.

"What proof have we," demanded Grim, "that if Mr. Meldrum Strange surrenders he won't be murdered?"

"No proof. Absolutely none. We never offer proof. We simply keep our promises. Never fail to do that. Never, never. That's all the trouble with that man Strange; we promised we'd get him if he didn't accept the offer that was made him, and we'll do it; you needn't doubt that for a minute. We'll certainly do it. If we broke promises there'd be no fear of us or faith in us."

"Are you authorized to make promises?" Grim asked him.

"Oh, no, not at all. I'm working my way in, you know. I'm what we call a gentleman cadet. You see, I had influence of the best sort, being the great Poulakis's nephew."

"Knew awkward secrets I suppose?" Grim suggested.

"Oh, yes. I knew a thing or two. But that wouldn't have helped. It was even a disadvantage. But the family connection helped to offset that. Oh, that's no secret; every one in Cairo knows my influence. I get more practice than perhaps you'd think."

"Practice?"

"Oh yes. I'm a lawyer. Believe me, I win cases for the right people. If the people who are slated to lose bring a case to me, I tell them I'm too busy and send them elsewhere."

"Why should Mr. Meldrum Strange marry Madame Poulakis?" Grim demanded. "Wouldn't settlements be enough without that?"

"Oh dear no. We find wives for all the big fish that come into our net. They'll make me marry, when I'm strong enough to be dangerous. The rule is that you mustn't trust a man without a woman to keep him from turning honest. So many men, you know, get sentimentally moral as they grow successful."

"Madame Poulakis is considered strong enough to manage Mr. Meldrum Strange?"

"Oh certainly. But, if you want my candid opinion, she's a bit of a handful for them as things are. She's inclined to be romantic, and that's the deuce. All Cairo has heard of her goings-on. She believes in esoteric foolishness. Keeps an Indian magician to study the stars and do hocus-pocus. I've heard a story about her being in love with Meldrum

Strange. No doubt she wants to be the wife of an American millionaire, and that would suit our people finely. We're invading the United States this year, you know."

"You want Mr. Meldrum Strange to go back there and work for you?"

"Yes, that's it. He'd be heavy artillery, wouldn't he! Of course, as I told you, I'm not in the inner council, only a gentleman cadet. We have cadets, too, who aren't gentlemen, but they never learn anything except how to do the rough work. The five who were with me tonight were Plain cadets. They just do what they're told. The highest promotion they can get is to be master-craftsmen; except that there's said to be one grand-master-craftsman who is on the inner council. But I don't really know about that; only members of the inner council know who the inner council really are."

"Fortunate we caught you, isn't it!" said Grim.

"For me, yes. Not for you, unless you're sensible. Your only chance of escaping with your lives is to be sensible and yield. We never fail to keep our promises."

"How d'you make it out fortunate for you that we caught you?" Grim demanded.

"Well, you see — that's obvious, isn't it? I was sent out tonight to get you. If I'd gone back with a failure against me, I expect that would have been the end of my prospects. But if I deliver you alive they'll consider me for a more important post. I'm glad to have this chance to talk with you. You can kill me, but that won't help you. You can take me back with you to Cairo, perhaps, and lodge me in the jail — also perhaps; but I think you would never reach Cairo. If you do reach Cairo, you can report all I've said; somebody will write down your statement with his tongue in his cheek, and you can all four solemnly swear to it. Unofficially quite a number of people will believe you, because you will be telling what quite a number of people know. But the newspapers will say you are mad, and officially your story will be described as a mere mare's nest. Also, you will die. Our agents are everywhere."

"Whereas, if Mr. Meldrum Strange surrenders?" Grim suggested.

"Ah! Then it is equally simple. If he surrenders and gives proper guarantees, there will then be initiation. Once initiated, he may recommend you others. If recommended, you will be given a chance to prove your availability. But if he prefers not to recommend you, you will be killed, of course, in order to protect him."

"What is the use of listening to you, if you're not allowed to make promises?" Grim asked him.

"I am allowed to accept the surrender of Meldrum Strange."

At that he raised his voice, and his eyes sought those of Meldrum Strange among the shadows.

"Let Meldrum Strange take a leaf out of our book," he said slowly. "Let him remember promises. I'm told that once in New York he kissed Madame Poulakis and said to her, 'When you're tired of your crook of a husband, come to me. I'm single.' They tell me Meldrum Strange has never married. What a romance for him! What an adventure! I wish I were in his shoes!"

Grim thought a minute, in the way a man studies a chess-board, taking his chin in his left hand.

"Give me that torch, and take him out of earshot, Jeremy," he said at last.

So Jeremy took our prisoner by the shoulder and shoved him out under the Granite Leaf, through the so-called anteroom into the Grand Gallery, whispering out of the corner of his mouth as he handed the torch to Grim —

"Cast my vote, Jim."

Grim waited until Jeremy's whistle announced that he had reached the farther end of the Grand Gallery; but he had already made his mind up, and his face as he went and leaned his back against the sarcophagus was a picture of satisfied amusement. "How about it, Strange?" he asked. "If Grim, Ramsden, and Ross agree to join this hunt with you, are you game to surrender to that gang and track things down to a conclusion?"

CHAPTER VIII

"Indiscreet subjected to sympathy."

MELDRUM STRANGE hesitated palpably. He didn't like handing over to Grim the direction in general, which was what Grim's proposal amounted to. I don't think he was afraid of being killed; but he didn't enjoy the possibility of being found with proof on his person of connection with crooks. Obviously, if ever the crooks should begin to suspect him, their simplest course would be to expose him and leave the law to take its course.

"You see," said Grim, making the flashlight dance on the ancient wall in front of him, "the only possible way to destroy this organization is from the inside. Their strength must lie in having accomplices in government departments. So if we join them and try to protect ourselves at the same time by informing the authorities, some spy in a high place is sure to give our game away. It's the whole hog or nothing. Either quit, and escape with our lives — which I think I can show you how to do; or turn our backs on society and plunge right in, trusting to clear ourselves at the proper time. My advice to you, Strange, is to back out of it and run for cover. That's personal; man to man."

"I won't do that," Strange answered, beginning to chew one of his cigars. "I suppose we could take the High Commissioner into our confidence."

Grim laughed.

"He'd put the hat on the whole thing right away. Imagine yourself High Commissioner. Imagine an American millionaire coming to you with any such proposal. Think what a fix you'd be in if he should get scuppered, with the U.S. newspapers roaring for your blood, and the members of this secret gang working to prove that the dead millionaire was really responsible for all the sins of Egypt! You would tell the millionaire to get out of the country quick. You made a bad break consulting him yesterday, if you don't mind my talking frankly."

"Then you propose to join this gang?"

"Exactly. There has got to be a point of contact. You can't catch fish on dry land. You can't squelch crime from an armchair. You've got to dig down in."

"Good enough, but Hell, you heard what was said about guarantees. They'll expect me to commit a murder, or something like that.

"They'll know you wouldn't take to murder. They know human nature. They'll have everything arranged. Depend on it, if you accept their terms, they'll take a first mortgage on your freedom, as well as considerable cash. And after that, if one of us makes one false step, 'Mafeesh — finish!' as the Arabs say. Watch your step, Strange!"

We discussed the pros and cons for half an hour; and little by little, what with the ancient mystery of the place with its four smoke-blackened, hand-rubbed granite walls that have stood for five thousand years without as much as hinting at their purpose, the excitement of fighting in that ancient place, and all his determination that had brought him as far as Egypt on a quixotic mission, Strange did what was inevitable.

"I'll go you, Grim," he said at last. "I've no family to speak of; only distant relatives, who'll contest my will if I don't outlive them. There are clubs I belong to that — oh, well, all that looks rather small from this distance. Call your friend Jeremy. I'll go you."

So I whistled and Jeremy drove Poulakis junior along in front of him, taking the flashlight back from Grim and turning it on each of our faces. He didn't need to ask questions. Neither did Poulakis.

"How should I communicate with Madame Poulakis?" Strange demanded.

"Easily!" Poulakis answered perkily. "Send me. If you were to leave this pyramid without sending me in advance, you would never reach Cairo alive, you know. Even if I were with you, that wouldn't help. They'd kill me too! The only thing is for me to let the right people know that you've surrendered at discretion."

"How do you propose to return to Cairo?" Strange demanded.

"Well, I shall not use your car, for it will not be there. By the way, you owe me for the hire of that car. I paid the man two pounds and sent him off, so as to get him out of the way. I expected to recoup myself out of your pockets after we had shot you. I have saved you three pounds; you had agreed to pay him much too much. Suppose you liquidate the obligation; honor between thieves, you know!"

It was as good as a show to see Strange battle with emotion as he peeled two 1-pound notes off a wad and passed them over. He enjoyed it about as much as a missionary would like putting wood under a cannibal's cooking pot, and Grim turned his face away to hide a smile. But Jeremy jumped to the occasion, establishing himself firmly in the good opinion of Poulakis junior.

"Match you for it!" he said instantly. "Come on. I'll toss you for the two pounds!"

Jeremy's silver coin hung in the air. Poulakis cried "Heads!" and Jeremy gave him two more pounds, hardly glancing at the coin as he caught it.

"Again — double or quits!" he insisted, and this time it was Poulakis who spun a coin; but Jeremy cried "Tails," and it was Jeremy who caught it in mid-air, and displayed it in his palm head-upward. He passed over two more pounds.

"I've only one pound left," he said then. "Want to toss for that?"

Poulakis won. Jeremy paid with a laugh. Grim took the flashlight and led the way out into the Grand Gallery, Jeremy falling behind to whisper to Strange and me.

"Let that sort of snipe think you're a gambler and he's easy forever after. Play high and lose to 'em. Nothing makes 'em trust you sooner. Let's all bet like the Devil whenever we think we're being watched. Show the cash. We can straighten up afterward."

If Jeremy could have his way, the world would be run like a Gilbert and Sullivan opera, with Jeremy flitting from pillar to post uncovering laughs as swiftly as the audience could stand it. We agreed to become gamblers.

At the foot of the first ascending passage the blood had almost vanished, soaked up in the limestone dust. There was no sign of a dead man, although there was blood on the floor of Al-Mamoun's tunnel, where the rifle-volley had just missed us and caught our opponents. Our assailants had sneaked in and carried away their fallen. Moreover they had gone, for the pyramid entrance was blocked by the Arab guides, who clamored for their money, demanding ten times what they had bargained for because of what had taken place. Poulakis himself drove a bargain with two of them to carry him as far as the Mena House Hotel "because the sand might get into his shoes."

So they bore him off, we continuing to sit there yawning, watching the dawn rise mauve and golden, watched in turn by the remainder of the guides. We didn't propose to pay them as long as they would sit there and protect us by their presence from another surprise attack, any more than they proposed to let us out of arm's reach until they had our money.

And you know, the dawn makes an awful lot of difference to the aspect of a plan. Be as enthusiastic as you choose within four walls in the dark, you'll need to be a man of iron resolution to feel the same way outdoors in the early morning. The earth begins to look more real, and the ideas visionary. Difficulties, that in the dark were part of the dark and as intangible and vague, grow raw and real in daylight.

If any one had come to us then with an ounce of common-sense persuasiveness I believe he could have talked even Grim into abandoning the plan within five minutes.

But no one came who had any interest in changing our course, and none of us cared to hoist the white feather, so we sat there in as deep silence as the Arab guides permitted — which is to say in the midst of a crows' chorus — until the two who had carried Poulakis came back to tell us that a car was waiting for us near the Mena House Hotel. Even so, we didn't pay them until they had accompanied us all the way to the Mena House, and seen us into the car. They formed a fine unconscious body-guard, and we were sorry to leave them.

The car was a truly magnificent affair, with leopard-skin robes and a driver who outshone any darky ever seen in the States. All traffic rules — if there were any — went by the board, and we drove to meet destiny at fifty miles an hour, bellowing through a horn like Gabriel's trumpet to the early farmer-folk to clear the ways. They cleared it, too, right into the ditch quite frequently, being used to the ways of the Egyptian pasha.

I really don't know what we expected — what we supposed our destination was. I had a vague notion that we were on the way to Madame Poulakis's palace where conspiracy would be already working full blast. But that was leaving Egypt out of the reckoning. Few criminals are habitually early risers.

We were taken straight to Shepheard's Hotel, where the only suggestion of intrigue was two scented envelopes handed to Grim by a sleepy Sudanese porter, who professed not to know who had brought them. The first was from Madame Poulakis, addressed to us all:

You dears, how happy I am! I have sat up waiting for the news and fearing the worst! How I congratulate you! And myself! And all of us! Mon dieu, how you must be tired and sleepy, for I can hardly keep my own eyes open, yet you must have spent ten nights in one. So rest yourselves. This evening must find you well recovered. It is with delight that I accept your kind invitation to dine with you. As I shall take such advantage of your kindness as to bring three friends, please perfect your generosity by inviting Meldrum Strange to your dinner to meet me! After the dinner, if agreeable, we will all attend a little rendezvous chez moi.

Yours most cordially, Z.

The second was from Narayan Singh, written in a much more sober hand than his former communications.

To Major J.S. Grim, the respectful salaam of Sepoy Narayan Singh. Jimgrim, sahib,

Fortune that forever favors your honor's interest sent me to this house suitably drunk, in which condition brain is too torpid to expel what enters ears, and eyes are too slumberous to avoid seeing things not meant to see. Subject your approval, shall continue to debauch, disposing of drink and drugs unofficially but accumulating official intoxication. Key to situation is Memsahib, who might prove indiscreet if subjected to sympathy. Details of little affair in Gizeh already known to many people. There are several spies in the hotel, but small danger until this evening, when the memsahib will attend dinner with other memsahibs appointed to prevent indiscretion. Much murder, including memsahib and all of us, will definitely take place after midnight unless plans regarding Strange sahib work without hitch.

In haste, Your honor's obedient servant, Narayan Singh.

"Damn it! Is that Sikh for us, or against us?" Strange demanded, passing the letter back to Grim.

Grim answered. "He has the eastern view-points," Grim answered. "He'll not respect western squeamishness. But he's one of us, first, last, and all the time!"

CHAPTER IX

"I understand you have changed sides!"

IT WASN'T any use sitting there wondering what Narayan Singh might mean by "indiscreet if subjected to sympathy." We disgusted the hotel folk by ordering light breakfast, and went to bed as soon as we had swallowed it, doubling up for extra safety. Then we disgusted the hotel folk a second time by insisting on lunch at three o'clock. So far we might have been prepaid tourists, seeing sights in the sweat of our brows.

But three-thirty brought an ambassador on the wings of impudence, if that's the right name for an imported, sporty-model car painted maroon and yellow, with a brace of pug-nosed Egyptian pages in the rumble up behind. And Lord, how that ambassador did like himself!

We were sitting on the veranda in cane armchairs when he approached, doffing his imported straw hat daintily and pulling off his yellow, imported gloves. He wiped his fore-head with an imported silk handkerchief that smelt of imported opopanax, lifted the knees of his London trousers to display his Paris socks, and sat down uninvited in the chair in front of us. Them he smiled to show his nice white imported American teeth, and waited for us to say some-thing. We said nothing, all four of us simultaneously and with one mind.

He consulted his gold wrist-watch; but if he meant that

for a hint we didn't take it. As he polished his finger-nails with the inside of a glove he kept looking at Strange as if expecting him to speak first.

I never saw a man I liked less. I think he had rouge on his cheeks, although I won't swear to that; it may have been a high complexion resulting from a little admixture of Hamitic blood. There was a dark, suggestive iris on the finger-nails he polished so thoughtfully that entitled him to the benefit of the doubt regarding rouge.

What made the effeminacy worse was an evident strength of physique. He had a swordsman's wrist and was wiry from head to heel, packing none of that fat under the ribs that makes most Cairenes over thirty years of age incapable of serious exercise.

His face was sly and arrogant — the face of a rascal who understands human weakness and habitually trades on it — almost classical at the first glance, totally repellent the second. You could see he was confident of possessing influence, contemptuous of all who might lack it, but really brave or courageous never.

No man possessing his combination of inquisitive nose, cruel mouth, and yellowish eyes that strip naked whatever they see, could sell me a quarter for twenty-five cents, let alone get information from me. But he was used to being treated with great respect, and our silence rattled him.

"A little different to our last meeting in New York, isn't it, Mr. Strange?" he said at last, with a hint of a sneer in his unexpectedly musical voice. I guess he sang love-songs to a guitar in his less inhuman moments. "You remember me, of course?"

"I remember kicking you out of my office," Strange answered.

"No need to tell you, then, that I am Andrieff Alexis. I propose that we take the rough-handling to which you were subjected last night as tit for tat, and call the personal score even, Mr. Strange. Is that agreeable to you?"

Strange growled something or other half under his breath and went on chewing one of his cigars, sitting back with his stomach out and both hands gripping the arms of the chair. It was surprising that with all that stomach for handicap he had been able to throw out such a man as this who called himself Alexis. Maybe it gave a true line on the latter's courage.

"Good. Let us call that balanced, then. I understand you have changed sides."

Strange made no answer. I began to suspect that Alexis was putting a bold front to a weak position, and the glint in Grim's quiet eyes confirmed my guess.

"You see," he went on, "we don't allow personal quarrels among members. Before a new member can be admitted there is inquiry into such questions as whether any member has a grudge against him. Unless I were to give my personal assurance on that score you couldn't be approved. People who apply for admission but fail to be approved are put out of the way. I made up my mind to do the handsome thing and call on them to bury the hatchet."

At that Strange showed his caliber. He seized the upper hand.

"I guess you mean your mind was made up for you," he retorted. "You're not the kind of person who gets kicked and forgives it. Your organization made war on me because they want my help. They won't let such a little matter as your personal feelings stand in the way of my joining them. That's what brings you here, now isn't it?"

"I assure you —"

"No use your assuring me of anything! I challenge your authority to represent any one except yourself!"

"Oh, very well," Alexis answered. "If you prefer to keep on quarreling —"

"Quarreling?" said Strange. "Ten men like you couldn't quarrel with me! If you want to make your peace with me, you can do it by taking care not to offend me in future."

Alexis showed his false teeth in a smile that was meant to suggest resources in reserve, but it hardly hid exasperation.

"Well," he said after half a minute, "we've no use, of course, for sentiment. Nobody expects you to kiss me on both cheeks. I accept your statement that you have no personal quarrel with me. I have none with you. My dealings with you have been official. Your assault on me in New York was therefore as impersonal as that of one soldier on another on a battlefield. I am glad you appreciate that. But let me tell you something, by way of warning; a rule of our society is that members must submit their personal differences to a committee of three, whose decision is absolute. A new member who picked a quarrel with one of long standing would be sentenced to death. A case of that sort happened recently to my knowledge."

"Is my understanding correct that I am to be passed on for membership tonight?" demanded Strange.

"I believe perfectly correct."

"Will you be present?"

"Er — no. No, I imagine not."

"Umph! You have to report to some one, though, that you've made your peace with me?"

"I shall do that presently."

"Very well. Will you carry a message from me?"

"I am willing to repeat it."

"Tell 'em this, then. If there's to be peace it's between your organization and mine. These men you see with me are members of my organization. They come in with me or I stay out. There's nothing to argue about."

"But you're in no position to dictate on what terms you will come in," Alexis answered rather hotly. "We're self-perpetuating; we select our membership."

"That's my message," Strange retorted, "They come in with me, or I stay out."

"I will convey your message."

"I assure you —"

Alexis sat fanning himself with an ivory-handled, horse-tail fly-switch. I think he expected us to offer him a drink. At the end of three or four minutes' silence he got up, doffed his wonderful straw hat very gracefully, and drove away in the maroon-and-yellow car with the exhaust wide open to call attention to his finery.

Grim nodded. "Excellent! He'll report every word of that!"

"We're being watched," said Jeremy. "Gamble. Quick!"

We began to play "Two tip," Australian style, betting in pounds and fives and tens on every toss of the coin. Lord knows how many hundred pounds of Strange's money changed hands in twenty minutes, for it's amazing how the luck runs when you mean to return your winnings afterward. We were hard at it, when another individual crossed from the far end of the veranda and took the chair vacated by Alexis. Grim glanced once at him and kicked my shin. I nudged Strange and Jeremy. We stopped the game and ordered whisky-and-soda, which gave the new arrival an opportunity to show his hand. He looked like an Englishman who had been drilled — perhaps a retired Army officer.

"I wish you men would invite me to drink with you," he said suddenly. "I've just come here from Kantara on purpose to talk with you and I don't want to attract attention."

We obliged him and he studied all the other people on the veranda rather dramatically before broaching his subject.

"My name is supposed to be McAlister," he began then, sipping slowly at his drink. "You, I believe, are Mr. Meldrum Strange and Mr. Ramsden, Americans; Major Grim, also an American but of the British Army; and Mr. Jeremy Ross, Australian. Am I right?"

There was a slight slip, but Grim didn't correct him; technically, perhaps, he still was of the British Army, and anyhow, it isn't wise to squander information at the first excuse.

"The Administration is quite familiar with most details of your present predicament," the man who called himself McAlister went on. "All that took place at the Pyramid last night is known. The Arabs reported it."

"Oh, I'm glad to hear that," said Grim. "What did they say took place inside?"

"They reported everything — told all about the fighting, and how you carried a man named Poulakis down to the King's Chamber. Everything's known."

Grim nodded — more to us than to him, and there was a

smile behind his eyes. Strange started chewing a new cigar. The Arabs weren't there when the fighting took place; they couldn't possibly have seen us carry off Poulakis, and that was all about it.

"It's understood, of course," he continued, "that your sole purpose is to expose this gang. I've been brought special to Cairo to get in touch with you and act as liaison officer between you and the Administration. So if you'll take me into confidence, we'll set a trap for this gang and catch the principals."

Grim shook his head. " 'Fraid not," he answered. "After what took place last night, we'd be afraid. It seems perfectly clear to us that the Administration police are honeycombed with crookedness, and we've decided to let things take their course."

"Well, at least you'll give evidence?" asked McAlister with an air of being scandalized.

"I guess not," Grim answered. "We'd only get murdered. We prefer to live."

McAlister said no more, but swallowed the remainder of his drink and walked away.

"Page one, chapter one of our initiation," Grim remarked when he was out of earshot.

"Clumsy stuff!" Strange added.

"The funny part is," said Grim, "that I know that fellow. I've a long memory for names and faces. His real name is Smith. He was cashiered out of the Army for misappropriating money, and I suppose the poor devil picks up a living however he can. He's no insider. He hasn't brains enough to be."

The next man they sent to test us was more dangerous. He was an honest-to-goodness Government official, with the title of pasha and a suitably worried air — a neat, nice-looking little man, wearing a red *tarboosh* but otherwise dressed in European style; and in order to establish his identity beyond all question, he had one of the hotel under-managers come and introduce him to us.

"Ibraim Noorian Pasha!"

He accepted a cigarette, lighted it nervously, and smoked for a minute or two with his knees close together and his ebony cane laid over them; damned diffident he was.

"Hem! I am a department secretary. Police department. No, nothing to drink. Ahem! That affair last night. At the Pyramid. Disagreeable business. Going altogether too far. We shall get a bad name here in Egypt. Ahem! No sooner self-government in sight than things like this happen. Won't do! No. It must be stopped. Hellish individuals spoiling the future for everybody else. Spoiling everything.

"What do you propose?" asked Grim.

"Ahem! Delicate matter." His voice, too, was delicate. He had delicate brown eyes that kept you thinking of a mouse. "Quite frankly, I'm taking my life in my hands to talk to you."

"Oh, nonsense!" answered Grim.

"No, not nonsense! Unfortunately the police are totally corrupt. Can't depend on any one. All the fault of the English. Things completely out of hand. A few of us might straighten matters out, if we had assistance. Ahem! I want you gentlemen to help me — confidentially. Quite confidentially. We have spies. Police department spies. They bring us information. Ahem! The rascals who attacked you last night hope to get you to go to America. Work for them there. Bold people. Agents everywhere. Quite too many for us, unless we get assistance. Police need people like you. Now — ahem! Why don't you pretend to agree with them? Then expose them to us? I'm quite frank with you. I'm hoping for reformation that would almost be revolution in the police department. A coup such as that would promote me to be head of the department. We would have a practically new police force in no time. I can guarantee your protection meanwhile. Ahem! Will you do it?"

"No!" said Grim. "I don't believe in your police protection. How much were we protected last night?"

At that Ibraim Noorian Pasha taxed us with supine immorality. "The white races are growing degenerate!" he announced with an air of pained conviction. But Grim uncovered the weakness of his position.

"If you don't like our attitude why don't you arrest us as material witnesses?" he asked.

"Pffaah. The English would order you released immediately."

And he got up and left us, walking away in a fine fit of assumed anger with his *tarboosh* set at an angle that made him look like a bantam rooster.

"Here endeth the second lesson!" announced Jeremy.

Nothing further transpired until we dressed for dinner and came down again to the veranda to await Madame Poulakis and her friends. There is no limit to Egyptian surprises. They came half an hour ahead of the appointed time in two closed carriages that wouldn't have looked badly at a coronation. Up on the platform behind the front carriage stood no other than Narayan Singh, sober as a judge, gorgeous in new turban, and silk from shoulder to heel, with a scimitar, if you please, tucked into the sash at his waist. It was he who got down to open the carriage door and escort Madame Poulakis up the hotel steps.

We had ordered a special dinner. There was no use going to the dining-room at once, for it wouldn't be ready. The three women whom Madame Poulakis had brought were married, if rings on their hands meant anything, and well used to being waited on hand and foot with all the luxuries. "Cocktails in a corner! Who'll play?" asked Jeremy, striking an attitude — and they would all play, obviously.

Jeremy led the way to a corner lounge, and Grim managed to get a word to me.

"Cairene women are never punctual," he said. "There's purpose in this. Suppose you walk right on through and see whether Narayan Singh doesn't follow you."

MAKING no excuses, I shoved both fists into my jacket pockets and strolled through to the palm garden. There I sat down on a bench beyond the big fountain in the center, with both eyes lifting to make sure there were no spies in close attendance. It is in just such simple ways that fish escape from nets and plots crack open. Nobody paid any attention when Narayan Singh, dressed as a servant, followed me through the hall ostensibly toward the rear where he belonged. He came straight to where I was waiting, and sat down beside me.

"*Sahib,*" he said, "our Jimgrim has a dangerous friend in Meldrum Strange. It is all one to the gods whether a man is drunk or sober, and at times they need a drunken man. Yesterday in the very early morning I was drunk. But the whisky was good, and I only had a bottle of it. I rang for more, but the black *badmash* who answered told me impudently that the bar was shut; so, being wrathful and indignant at such limitations, I set the furniture outside on the veranda, leaving a naked room, and went out in search of some place where conviviality knows no limit and a man's thirst isn't held answerable to the clock.

"But they run this city like an army canteen, *sahib!* I walked far, but found no liquor. And having found fault with an Egyptian policeman, who refused to direct me to an open drinking-place, and who blew his whistle lustily from underneath the garbage in a night-cart into which I thrust him to teach him manners, I set out to put great distance between this hotel and me, not wishing that you *sahibs* should be disturbed on my account.

"So I crossed the Nile by a bridge, cursing the water for being unintoxicating stuff; and if curses have value, *sahib,* the Nile in its next life will be a sewer flowing in the dark under unclean city streets! Ever seeking whisky, I walked on and on, not drunk enough to be unreasonable, but with a certain ardor in my veins for conquest and the clash of forces. My intellect was alert and rational, for I recalled that I spoke to myself in English, French, and German as I walked along; but my heart had the mastery, and intellect could only serve the heart that night. First I desired more whisky; but after that I longed above all else to find a damsel in distress and to smite her enemies. At that hour the gods had use for a man exactly in that mood!

by Talbot Mundy

"There was a fracas, *sahib,* a fracas in the dark, and it was music to me! I approached a house that resembled nothing else so much as one of those new palaces our fat, degenerate rajahs build — a pastry-cook's delirium, made up of all new fashions blended, with sufficient of the old to cause the lot to ferment like indecency within an old man's body. Phaugh! A house of money without brains! There was a great carriage outside this abortion of a house, and a woman within it screaming; so I came swiftly.

"No fewer than nine men, *sahib* — for they seem to call such creatures by the name of men in Egypt — were endeavoring to drag this woman from the carriage. And another woman helped them, while only two men took the other side, and they timidly, using more voice than violence. All this I saw as I came upon them, thinking how I might best apply my strength and whatever skill I may have picked up in course of a few campaigns.

"It was nothing to me what those Egyptians wanted with the woman, but a very great deal it meant to stand between them and their desire. I burst on them as a typhoon smites the trees. I hurled, flung, smote! I threw them under the horses! I trod men underfoot. To their eyes I must have seemed to be a dozen men! I was swift, crashing their heads together, attacking now this and then that one, aided a little at last by the coachman and footman, who took courage.

"The other woman ran. I know not what became of her. She may have entered the house. A fool aimed a pistol at me dwelling on the trigger and I ducked. I seized him around the belly, he firing as I lifted him. I flung him under the horses, hoping they would tread him into red mud, and what with his carcass striking their forelegs, and the pistol-shot, the horses, which were mettled beasts, took fright and bolted, but not before the coachman had scrambled up and seized the reins.

"The gods take charge of a man's intellect in moments such as that, *sahib.* I was minded neither to remain and defend myself against the men, nor to forego the acquaintance of that lady in the carriage, who might wish to acquire merit by thanking me for service rendered. So I seized the carriage and jumped in, she screaming. I doubt not that in the dark I was an apparition to terrify any woman, with my turban all awry amid one thing and another.

" 'O Queen,' said I, 'I will defend you against your enemies. There is no need to fear me at all.'

"And I sat on the front seat with my arms folded thus, that she might see I had no intention of affronting her. Even so in the dark I could see that she was young, and more beautiful than the moon and stars; and I thanked the thoughtful gods who had brought me there. I had just sufficient whisky in my belly to make me adventurous, without unsettling discretion. Clear, reasonable, discreet my mind was.

" 'O lady, I have sworn an oath this night to serve in future none but queens,' said I, 'so if you are not yet a queen, lo! I will make you into one. Trust me!' said I.

" 'If you have ten-thousand enemies, they shall die ten thousand deaths, one each, and that is all about it! Charge me with a service. Name but a deed, and I will do it!'

"So she bade me stop the horses, which were galloping pell-mell, we swaying this and that way like a big gun going into action, first this wheel and then that striking against a curb-stone as the coachman wrenched at the reins.

" 'If you could save us from an accident,' she said, 'by doing something that would stop the horses, that would be a kindness beyond words.'

"Well, *sahib,* that seemed a very little thing to me in the state of mind that I was in. I climbed out on to the driver's seat. I thrust aside the coachman, whose wits fear had taken from him, I leaped on the back of the near horse. I come of a race of horsemen, *sahib.* No pair of horses lives that can say 'yea' to my 'nay' for more than a minute or two. Presently they stopped, and I climbed back into the carriage, sitting as before with folded arms.

"By that time the lady had regained her self-command, and eyed me curiously rather than with fear. She began to question me, asking my name and who I might be; and I, not squandering truth as some men do when strong drink is in them, but inspired by the gods to tell the first lie that crossed my mind, said I was a deserter from the British Army.

"Whereat, *sahib,* she clapped her hands delightedly and offered me a place to hide, saying I should be her private bodyguard and strong protector. And I, caring nothing what the future should bring forth, would only that the present should continue interesting, fell in with her suggestion, protesting with great oaths that I would tear up Egypt by the roots at a word from her.

"And after a while we came to the palace in which you found me. There at the gate the carriage stopped, and the footman, who had ridden on the platform behind the carriage, opened the door and offered me insolence. I was minded to pull his head out by the roots, but she checked me in time to save his life. She said it would not look well for me to ride into the house inside the carriage with her so I sprang on the footboard. Thus we drove in, the footman walking, hugging at his throat where I had twisted it, and the great gate clanged behind us.

"So far, good. My walk had produced no whisky, but some amusement nevertheless. I was in a mood for great adventures, *sahib.* Said I: 'O queen, lead me to your apartment, that I may sleep in front of the door and guard you. Impudent devils who would try to drag you from your carriage would stop at nothing less than such an obstacle as me! These servants of yours are muzzled dogs that can't bite,' I said; and she laughed with no little reassurance.

"So we entered that palace in which you found me, and she led me to a great room like a chamber in paradise, overlooking the Nile, which nevertheless is no heavenly river. And she sent for Narendra Nath, an old fool of a Hindu soothsayer. His perpetual study is of all the world's religions. His wisdom is a patchwork of craziness. He is teller of fortunes. He had foretold to her that she would be attacked, as any child might have done, knowing already what Narendra Nath knew; for she tells him everything.

"Narendra Nath said that the gods had sent me, which is doubtless true. She bade me go with him and learn what is required of me, he saying to her in an undertone that a little drunkenness in the circumstances was no bad thing. My ears are sharp, *sahibs.* So I feigned greater drunkenness, behaving as one from whose brain the fumes of liquor are fading, which is a stage in which few men have their wits about them; and he took me to the room upstairs in which you found me, where certain bigger fools than he set up a wailing on wind instruments such as is never heard outside of India, and only there in the performance of certain secret rites during which they hypnotize the neophyte. None can hypnotize any man, *sahib,* who is not afraid to do his own thinking — which, I take it, is why the British govern India.

"Narendra Nath plied me with drugs, which he said would relieve my headache. But Jeremy *sahib* has been teaching me legerdemain, and I was able to palm the pills and make away with them. Nevertheless, observe, *sahib;* see how I can make my eyes grow large, as if drugs had dazed them. That is a muscular trick; I have used it to get into hospital at the end of arduous service, when I needed a rest and a change of diet.

"When he believed me under the influence of drugs and music, he sent for her; and they asked me questions about you *sahibs.* I left nothing unsaid in praise of you. I recalled a multitude of things that never happened. I magnified real deeds until they sounded like the miracles of gods. Then they asked me about Meldrum Strange; but knowing nothing about him, I said less than nothing, being satisfied to look perplexed.

" Too many men prefer to look wise, *sahib,* when they know nothing, which causes the sensitive gates of uncertainty to close on confidence; whereas a look of perplexity tempts indiscretion.

"So they told me about Meldrum Strange, believing me to

be hypnotized and receptive to all manner of suggestions. She told me how her husband had been a member of a society so secret that it has no name. And then Narendra Nath took up the burden of the tale, and told how the lady Poulakis had continued to be a member of the society, because of their rule that none may escape from membership except through the door of death.

" 'She is a bird in the net,' said he, 'too young to wish to die; too potentially useful for them to desire to kill her; yet doomed to death, unless she shall serve their present purpose.

" 'And their suspicions of her,' said he, 'are well founded. She is weary of this wicked business. She is anxious to be free from them, yet can find no way out of the net. So little do they trust her,' said he, 'that, as you yourself have seen, they sought to make her prisoner in another woman's house, where the pressure of tenfold fear could be brought to bear on her. Therefore, let your duty and your highest pleasure be to guard her day and night. Be devoted to her service.'

"To which I, speaking as a man who dreams, made answer that I am liable to be arrested for desertion; for it seemed to me, *sahib,* that that might open a way of communication with Jimgrim. As in truth it did. Later on, when they had well considered matters, they bade me write a letter, as you know.

"Then they had an argument as to whether they should tell me more, he taking the nay and she the yea of it, and she prevailing, as a woman will. 'His inner mind,' said she, 'is opened. It will be an inner secret, to be well kept, and will add to the inner impulse that governs his waking brain.' That is the way people argue, *sahib,* who have a smattering of occult knowledge.

"So she told me, Narendra Nath unwillingly consenting. Said she: 'I am required to marry Meldrum Strange, whom they seek to control for the purpose of great financial undertakings in America. Now I am not unwilling,' said she, 'to marry Meldrum Strange, having met him and not disliking him at all. He offers my one path of escape. But there is this great difficulty — he undoubtedly believes me to be a wicked woman, and he is the last man who would choose a wife from among a society of criminals. Yet unless he consents to marry me they will murder him. And unless I succeed in this matter they will murder me. So what can I do but protect myself, if that is possible, and hope for the best, and see what happens?'

"I made no answer to all that, *sahib,* being supposed to be in a sort of trance, and aware also that folk who made use of such practices believe themselves able to arouse all the wisdom hidden in the recesses of a man's inner mind, so that, although he cannot answer, being in a trance, he will none the less apply great wisdom to his conduct in the matter when the trance is ended.

"So then she retired to her apartment, and old Narendra Nath continued his schooling of me, suggesting to me that it were an act of wisdom to involve all you four *sahibs* in this matter, by persuading you to conceal my whereabouts, thus conniving at my desertion; by which means a certain hold over you might be obtained, with the aid of which a pressure could be brought to bear that might compel you to act on behalf of Madame Poulakis. But to tell the truth, *sahib,* the old man is at his wits' end, not knowing what to say or do, yet afraid to admit to them that his occultism and astrology and what not are of no avail.

"After a while it seemed good to him to put me into a deeper trance, which suited my convenience exactly. Life in the Army, *sahib,* is a matter of discipline, which has its profit as well as loss — profit of self-control to balance loss of liberty. Certain things are done at certain times, and a man who has the soldier spirit to begin with soon learns to sleep lightly and to wake himself, whether at the right time or at the first unusual sound. A little liquor makes no difference — not such a little as I had had. So I fell asleep with perfect confidence that I would wake when necessary. And so I did. But I awoke with only one eye open, and closed that almost instantly.

"There came into the room a heavy man of coarse build but with a voice like oil. He had puffy, white hands, with a large emerald ring on the right one; but I saw little else, for the first thing he did was to examine me.

" 'He is in a trance,' said Narendra Nath.

"But the man kicked me three times to make sure, putting me to the utmost exercise of self-control. I have prayed that I may break his neck for those three kicks he gave me. Never have I suffered sharper pain, even when wounded on the battlefield. Yet I lay still; and he believed I was in a trance.

" 'Who and what is he?' he demanded.

" 'Merely a madman,' said Narendra Nath. 'I have calmed him by the exercise of certain powers I possess.'

" 'Mad he must be!' said the other fellow. 'Is he that devil who made ninepins out of nine of us early this morning in the street and drove away in the Poulakis's carriage? The same, eh? And you have him hypnotized? Well, he has qualities that we can use to good advantage. You'd better pour some sense into his ear while he's in that trance. He'll make good gallows-meat. And another matter, while I think of it; what has come over the servants in this house? I had to threaten them before they'd admit me!'

"Narendra Nath swore he knew nothing about that; but the other threatened him with dire consequences if it ever should happen again. Said he:

" 'You're only allowed to live here as a spy on her. It's your business to see that her servants understand to whom to look for orders. She has been growing willful of late,' he said, 'and her servants follow suit.'

"Narendra Nath was very humble in reply, and then the other in a voice more oily than ever went on to say really why he had come.

" 'Cast her a new horoscope!' said he. 'Cast her a horoscope in which her second husband is an American millionaire. Make it clever. Let there be a dividing of the ways; if she takes the right hand way and becomes the American's wife, good; if she takes the other, and refuses, promise her a terrible death! Better hear voices, hadn't you? And one other thing; if Meldrum Strange should refuse he'll be too dangerous to leave at large. He'll have to be disposed of. We'll make use of this fool. Hypnotize him! Tune him up, and keep him tuned!'

"Then he went away, I seeing nothing but his back, which was not remarkable, except that his neck was thicker than ordinary, with a roll of fat protruding above the collar. And I slept on and off like a fox until evening."

CHAPTER X

"And, no boaster though I be —"

IT WAS past the dinner hour and Narayan Singh caught me looking at my watch.

"They will think I have gone to the servants' quarters, *sahib*. Madame Poulakis knows my real purpose. It is important to hear the end of this."

"Jimgrim will invent an excuse for me," I said. "Go on."

"Aye, trust him, *sahib*. Well, as I lay between sleeping and waking, I thought; for there was nothing else to do. And when the gods have use for a man they give him wise thoughts. So when Madame Poulakis came again and brought note-paper, and I wrote you the note that brought you to the house, I wrote a second note and hid it. That second note was the one that I slipped into your shoe. And at the same time I pretended to recover entirely from the trance and made no small fuss about being a deserter, who could be arrested and put in prison; so that they were all the more eager to get you here, and sent a carriage with the note.

"Then Narendra Nath gave me more drugs, and tried to put me to sleep again, she maintaining that you *sahibs* would insist on taking me away if I should be too sane in appearance. Moreover, I was of the same mind, and I did not wish to be taken away, having taken great pity on this woman, who flutters like a bird in the net. The gods had also put into my head a rather high opinion of Narendra Nath. The old man is a charlatan and practises much nonsense, but nevertheless he believes the half of what he says and persuades himself of the other half. Thought I: he loves her, and the poor old fool would help her out of the net if he could contrive it.

"And while I made believe to fall asleep, she cooked up with Narendra Nath a story to tell you *sahibs* that should account for my presence without disclosing secrets; for she and he are in terror of disclosing a hint of the secret society's doings. It was Narendra Nath's idea to have that music playing while you were in the house. He said it would help to bewilder your minds and make you amenable to the right suggestion. Men whose minds are superstitious are readily trapped in just such ways, and he did not know you are not superstitious.

"Well, *sahib;* after you had come and gone again, I spoke to old Narendra Nath as man to man. Said I, 'My father, you seem to me like one who struggles in a whirlpool, seeking to save another but unable to stem the current, which carries you round and round.' And he stared at me, making no answer.

" 'Furthermore,' said I, 'it must be plain to you that your sorcery doesn't always work, for here am I, who have deceived you easily, even while drunk. I have heard and I have seen all that took place in this room,' said I, 'and I know that you are an honest old man, in so far as you understand honesty, although not nearly as wise as you wish to believe. Whereas,' I told him, 'I not only am an honest man but a wise one also, the proof of which is that I became drunk when the gods wished!'

" 'You are not only an impudent trickster,' he answered me, 'but a conceited Sikh heretic as well!'

" 'Nevertheless,' said I, 'I crave to acquire merit by defending the distressed, which is the essence of the Sikh doctrine.'

"Said he, 'If I raise my voice there will come men, who are less merciful than any in your experience!'

" 'I, too, can be merciless,' I said. 'I gave nine of them a taste of my quality already, and no boaster though I be, I tell you this house will never hold enough Levantines to keep me prisoner should the gods once cause me to dislike the place. I am the father of typhoons,' said I, 'and I know four *sahibs,* all true friends of mine, who compared to me in cunning and strength and fury are as mammoths to a mouse!'

"Well, *sahib;* the old man stared at me, and began to think like a man instead of like an abstraction.

" 'There are five miscreants,' said he, 'who direct this present wickedness. They call them the executive committee. They have no books, nor any written rules or records, and it might be that if something were to happen to those five this whole accursed society might fall to pieces. This executive committee is, as it were, the neck between the body and the head of the thing. The head would die and the body would die if the neck were severed!'

"That was man's talk, but old Narendra Nath cannot remain a man, *sahib,* for too long at a time, since charlatanry grows into a habit. He closed his eyes and murmured for a while then, describing a vision he had seem of strangers from the East and from the West, who came and smote a devil with five heads, thus setting free her who is nearest to his old heart. I knew that he made up the vision even while he spoke, for that is the way of self-deception. Was I not born in India? Hah! My mother's uncle was just such an one as this Narendra Nath, forever seeing visions after the event and claiming to be a prophet!

"Then came Madame Poulakis again with news that you *sahibs* had been tracked to the Great Pyramid, where gun-men had doubtless already murdered you.

" 'And that means that they will next come and murder me,' she said, 'for they will think me of no further use, as well as dangerous.'

"But I reassured her on that point, saying that you *sahibs* are difficult men to murder, and moreover that first they must murder me before they can kill her. And instead of being shocked to discover that I had not been in a trance at all, she seemed overjoyed at it, declaring that she had found a man at last who has brains as well as courage!

"Then there came more news. I was thrust hurriedly behind that gilded screen, and the music-makers were sent away. Unseen, I could hear all and see a little. There came three men, he of the thick neck not among them, and the first, who had a little black beard of a sort some missionaries wear, said:

" 'Your future is yet before you, Madame Poulakis. Is it true that you are invited to dinner at Shepheard's Hotel? Then write a note of acceptance, with the request that Meldrum Strange be included in the party. Where is that drunken Indian?'

"They said I was very sick, and had been put to bed. Narendra Nath said darkly:

" 'He will recover. He is under the influence. It has seemed wise to me to attach him to Madame as personal servant. He will account for her, for I have found in him fine qualities of obedience and faithfulness, which can be trained into the proper channel.'

"They were pleased at that, *sahib;* for they understood him to mean that I would slay her at a word from Narendra Nath. And Madame Poulakis, who has a woman's quickness, made believe to be afraid of me. Whereat those three men, thoroughly believing Narendra Nath to be their tool, insisted that I shall be Madame's bodyguard, she consenting only with reluctance. Then said the man with the missionary's face:

" 'This man Strange has surrendered to us. We shall put him and his friends to various tests this afternoon, and if they do not walk into the traps, so that we believe their surrender to be genuine, then tonight there will be initiation.

" 'Thereafter you must marry him, Zelmira. Among the guarantees that we shall insist on will be the settlement of enormous sums on you. So we have brought these papers for you to sign now. They are cleverly drawn. They consist of records of various supposititious transactions of a financial nature extending over a period of years, resulting in a loss to you of more than a million pounds.

"You will sign these papers now, admitting liability; but you will say nothing about them to Strange. We shall require him to accept responsibility for your debts when he makes the marriage settlement; and when the proper time comes we shall collect, either from him, or from you, or from both of you. In the event of his death these papers would be extremely valuable.

" 'So make yourself attractive,' he went on, 'and after the dinner at the hotel bring him and his friends to the house you know of, where the Five will have a final session with him. If he agrees then to our terms, well and good — you will be married at the United States consulate tomorrow morning. But if we find flaws in his attitude, that will be the last of him and his friends — and incidentally of any one whose existence might make us nervous. You understand me, Zelmira?'

"And at that, *sahib,* one of the three piped up in a thin voice and asked what means would be used for making away with Strange and four others, if that should prove necessary. He said it would be hardly as simple as killing unknown men. And the man with the face like a missionary laughed.

" 'Did you never hear of Sarajevo?' he demanded. 'Who slew the Archduke of Austria? A fool of a fanatic. What about this Indian then? He came here from Syria with those friends of Meldrum Strange. What could be simpler than to have him kill them all? The safest tool that can be used is a religious fanatic, or an anarchist fanatic. Let Narendra Nath fill the Indian up with hashish and whisper the right suggestions to him. Then, even if some one else must do the actual killing, that won't matter; we can come out like honest men and accuse the Indian. What defense will he have? He will be an Indian who ran amok under the influence of hashish, and we will provide him with a lawyer at his trial, who will get him hanged as surely as we sit here!'

"They all seemed to agree that that was an excellent proposal, *sahib,* and after they had made Madame Poulakis sign those papers they went away. She became hysterical for a while, but Narendra Nath comforted her, and I made great boastings such as women love to hear. This afternoon they fitted me up with this livery you see. Do I look like a popinjay? Hah! I smell action, *sahib!* There will be blood on this scimitar before morning, or I am a poorer prophet than Narendra Nath! Tell me, *sahib:* of what is this Meldrum Strange made — iron or beeswax?"

"Iron," said I, "and not much rust."

"Good! Then get my news to Jimgrim, and all is well. But how to get the news to him? Those women who accompanied madame are spies."

I did not know how to answer him for wondering.

"There is a spirit in man —" That, and nothing else, occurred to me. Whoever wrote the Book of Job answered with another riddle any question you can ask about humans and their ways. How a Sepoy — a number on the muster-roll of the British Army, and drunk at that — should have been selected by what he called the gods to uncover evil, that was a mystery that seemed to dwarf all others at the moment.

We're taught to regard colored people as the agents of the enemy of man. Our missionaries go out to convert them, lest the heathen in their blindness overwhelm the world in another chaos any old night.

They've educated us, these missionaries have, into believing things that aren't so; and we commit the indecency, in consequence, of being astonished when a man with colored skin acts "white."

I ought to have known better. I was so surprised by the resourcefulness and courage of Narayan Singh, to say nothing of his wit, that I could hardly summon presence of mind enough to order him to the kitchen, while I went forward to devise some means of getting an account of his doings to Grim.

CHAPTER XI

"It's nice to know a millionaire who isn't wiser than the rest of us!"

IT WAS no easy matter to discover a means of getting Grim to leave the dinner-table without exciting comment or arousing the suspicion of the three women who had accompanied Madame Poulakis.

They were probably already exercised about my absence. In addition to that, there were probably spies keeping watch on us, who might, in fact, already have seen me talking with Narayan Singh, although I did not think so.

Guests entered the dining-room at Shepheard's from the corridor at one end, so that any one expecting me would watch in that direction. Our table was in mid-room, preserved from being conspicuous by a fountain and palms, which shut off the view of people coming in. I figured all that out, and looked for a side door opposite to where Jeremy was sitting. The door I selected was locked, but the gardener had left a hoe under some bushes near-by, and the lock came away without much noise or effort. I opened the door and stepped inside, finding myself behind a screen, as I expected. Watching from between the end of the screen and a palm, I could see our table, and particularly Jeremy, who faced me — was near enough, too, to hear almost every word that was said.

Being no respecter of sedateness or convention, Jeremy

was doing tricks with table-knives, producing day-old chicks out of napkins, and all that sort of foolishness. One of the guests at a near table had a huge dog lying beside him, and Jeremy used his ventriloquial gifts to make the beast talk, getting off comments on Egyptian society from what he called a "dog's-eye point of view." The attention of half the people in the room and of everybody at our table was fixed on him. But when Jeremy is doing tricks his own bright eyes are wandering everywhere, and it wasn't many minutes before he caught sight of me.

And he's quick, is friend Jeremy. He didn't check or falter in the patter he was reeling off — made no signal to me — glanced away, in fact — and finished the trick he was doing to an outburst of laughter and applause. It was his favorite old trick of pulling a live day-old chick in halves and making two of it, after producing chick number one in the first instance from a hard-boiled egg or a billiard ball.

"Oh, that's nothing," he said airily. "I know a much better one. But you'll believe I've had help if I let Grim sit at the table. I'll prove he isn't my accomplice. Grim, old top, suppose you go and hide behind that screen, where you can't see me and I can't see you. Don't come back till I call. It's going to take me several minutes to accomplish this. Now, watch my hands, everybody."

Grim got up with an air of thinking the whole business childish, and strolled over to the screen; but the instant he stepped behind it he was like a spring, coiled ready to go off.

"Quick! Spill it! What's the news?" he demanded.

Well, I tried to condense into a fifty-word telegram all that Narayan Singh had told me. Try it for yourself, and judge what luck I had! Jeremy saved the day by purposely blundering his trick and beginning all over again, calling out apologies to Grim for keeping him waiting.

"Now think!" I said when I had finished "and for the love of Mike tell me what to do; for I'll be blowed if I can figure it out."

I don't believe that men like Grim do think, as a matter of fact, on such occasions. It's a species of instinct or intuition, or both combined. Long experience and a habit of meeting emergencies combine to produce a state of mind that figures instantly, like one of those adding machines.

Grim glanced at the door I had come through, looked me full and fairly in the eye, and gave his orders — terse — quick — unmistakable — as if the automatic wheels inside his mind had cut them out of steel that instant.

"Let your eye follow a line diagonally across our table from Meldrum Strange to Jeremy. Carry straight on for twenty feet. Small round table. There sits Kennedy. Gray-haired man — evening dress — Intelligence Department — all alone. Go out here; come in the front way; make some excuse; sit down at his table. Tell him everything."

Promptly Grim returned to the dinner-table, resuming his bored expression, and I went out into the garden. All the way around the building I racked what brains I have for an excuse to approach this man Kennedy without arousing the suspicion of spies. I'm not a man who can walk into a public dining-room unobserved; I look bigger than ever in evening dress, and I was sweating with anxiety lest some stupidity of mine should upset Grim's calculations.

But I was reckoning without the other fellow, which I take it is the cause of ninety-nine per cent. of this world's difficulties. Kennedy got up and came to meet me the minute I entered the room — a lean-flanked man of fifty-five or sixty, with a sort of literary look due to his iron-gray hair and quiet manners. He had extraordinary bright eyes with heavy gray eyebrows, and a deep cleft in his chin.

But his most remarkable asset was a penetrating voice that he seemed to have in absolute control; when he first spoke, every word he said carried all over the room, but presently, when he reached his table and sat down, although to all appearance he was talking normally, and certainly didn't whisper, I don't believe the nearest waiter could have heard a word he said.

"You're Mr. Ramsden, aren't you? You can do me a favor, if you'll be kind enough. They tell me you've hunted elephants in the Lado Enclave. My leave starts tomorrow, and

I'm going there. Won't you sit at my table for half an hour and give me some pointers?"

I told him that my friends would have to be asked to excuse me first; so he took my arm, and made his own excuses to the party, begging for what he was pleased to call the "use" of me for half an hour. None of the women liked it, but they couldn't very well refuse, and Jeremy had their attention again almost before we had turned away.

The moment Kennedy and I sat down together I began on him.

"Grim has just told me to take you entirely into confidence," I said. "I don't know why. If you're off elephant hunting a thousand miles from here —"

"I'm not," he answered. "However, there's no hurry; wait until I've ordered you some wine and sent for your dinner to this table. I've been watching that little side-play behind the screen."

"I understand there are others watching," I warned him.

"No, I think not. There were five, just before dinner began; one waiter, a headwaiter, an ex-Englishman in evening dress, a Cairene cotton-jobber, and an Italian. They're in the lock-up. It's now eight-thirty. By nine o'clock your party — the men, I mean, yourself included, would also have been under arrest for your own protection unless one of you had made this move. Ever since Meldrum Strange called on the High Commissioner we've been considering some such step. We have Poulakis junior under lock and key, and fortunately we bagged him without any of his gang knowing anything about it. Caught him in the house of a woman whom he visits now and then, and locked them up together. She's an agent of ours. He talked."

So when the waiter had brought my dinner I talked too, telling Kennedy everything I knew about the whole affair, he laughing quietly most of the time, behaving, in fact, as if I were recounting reminiscences.

"Tell me," he said when I had finished, "do you know of any other nation than America that could produce a man like Meldrum Strange? The man is right, but not within his rights. What would you think of me, for instance, if I went to America and did there what he proposes to do here? However, it's too late to help that now. We've got to go forward. I'll say this for him; he has forced our hand, and personally I'm in his debt; I've been trying for months to bring this gang to book, but there was obstruction at headquarters. Tonight we're going to let the law go hang, act *ultra vires,* and feed these devils some of their own medicine. I'm likely to lose my job over it, but that doesn't matter, I'm about ready to retire. Out of a hundred and eighteen murders, we know of ninety in recent months that have been committed at the instigation of this gang or by its members. Can't prove a thing. If we bring them to trial there's no evidence. We shan't get the real ring-leaders tonight, but we'll get the five who call themselves executive committee, and let's hope they're ugly!

"No search-warrants. Didn't dare apply for them. Information would have leaked out. We've got a special, hand-picked force made up entirely of British officers, who've no connection with the police. They're supposed to be on their way to a party; and if they should suddenly become a rescue party, that would possibly not involve the Administration in a breach of its own laws. Individually the officers may find themselves in rather hot water, but they're willing to run that risk for the sake of rendering a public service."

"Where are the officers now?" I asked him.

"In this room."

I looked about me. There were twenty or thirty officers in uniform dining at different tables — no unusual number. You would never have suspected them of being there with a common purpose. There were not more than two dining together, and they were of various ranks, from major downward.

"Tell me," said I, "have you had any communication with Grim about this business?"

He chuckled. "No. Grim's an old crony of mine. We all know Grim in the Intelligence. When he sent in his resignation we wondered. When we saw him linking up with

Meldrum Strange we knew. Grim's an old war-horse — answers to the trumpet. Can't help himself — goes for the heart of trouble automatically like a needle to a magnet. Grim saw me on the job once yesterday and twice today — spotted me here as soon as he entered the room — saw that head-waiter taken in charge by one of my men — and possibly drew his own conclusions. However, we've discussed elephants long enough. Suppose you join your friends. Just go ahead with the evening's performance. Protect that Poulakis woman if you can; she's in danger. They'll suspect her of having betrayed them. Don't be surprised by anything that happens!"

So I JOINED our party, and was aware of being suspected by the women. None of the three was in the Poulakis class. They had neither her charm nor her well-bred self-control; they laughed too noisily, ate too greedily, and laid a lot too much emphasis on their own importance, besides making jokes about Strange and Zelmira Poulakis that would have been in rotten bad taste in any circumstances. It was difficult not to laugh at Strange, for he was getting red under the collar and almost ready to explode.

Nobody was drinking much. We laughed through dessert with Jeremy until the dark-eyed woman sitting on my left began hinting that it was time to go. Then, and not until then, Zelmira Poulakis began to betray signs of nervousness, mastering herself with difficulty, looking suddenly much older, and apparently at a loss for words. However, she managed to smile, and to make the next move gracefully.

"Now for the experience of your lives!" she said. "You will learn that this dinner has been a delightful overture to Grand Opera — Faust, let us say, for you are going to meet Mephistopheles!"

Narayan Singh came forward to meet us in the hall, looking solemn and magnificent in all that finery, and escorted Zelmira Poulakis to the carriage as only an Indian can. He induced the impression that she was a semi-deity, in whose footsteps flowers should spring up presently;

whereas the rest of us were merely to be tolerated, on the ground that she had condescended to acknowledge us. I suspect that half the reason why aristocracy is dying out is that impresarios as skillful as Narayan Singh are scarce in these days; a woman or man on social stilts needs a clever rogue to go in front and provide the proper atmosphere. On the way out I tried to speak to Grim, but one of the three chaperones spotted it and prevented by coming between us. It was her suggestion that he should ride in the front carriage with the women, and Grim couldn't well refuse.

Looking back as we drove away I saw automobiles assembling in the dark in front of the hotel steps, and not long afterward we began to be pursued at a distance by the purring of six or eight cars. One passed us, and stopped to let us pass again under pretext of a stalled engine; but the others kept well to the rear, trusting to the first to keep us in view.

We drove over the Nile and past the Poulakis mansion, down two or three streets to another house bigger than hers, standing gloomy and aloof with its sides all wan in moonlight. The shadow of one tree fell in the shape of a human skull across the front of it, and the urns on the pillars of the great gate looked like those you see over a cemetery wall. It was a perfect house for the sort of performance we were in for.

"Close enough to the Nile for dumping corpses without unnecessary scandal," as Jeremy sweetly expressed it. "Feel like a swim, you fellows? How about it, Strange? They tell me swimming with your throat cut's easy — no work to it — just drift down with the stream!

"Have we all got guns?" he demanded, as we drove in through the echoing gate and it clanged shut. Strange had none. I offered him mine and he refused it testily, for his nerves were on edge.

"No use for one," he answered. "Out of my line. I was a fool to bring you fellows on this errand. Save yourselves if there's any trouble, and —"

"Sure you're a fool!" laughed Jeremy, "but we like you, Strange, old top. It's nice to know a millionaire who isn't wiser than the rest of us! Here we are! Now for act one!" But they kept our carriage waiting several minutes before the first moved on and let ours draw up opposite the front door.

CHAPTER X

"Crooks are just crooks."

I WONDER how many men there are who can go forward into the unknown without making mental pictures in advance of what's coming. I believe Grim can. I know I can't. It may be that ability to refrain from "imagining vain things" leaves you free to imagine truly and successfully. We who imagine in advance form judgments in advance and I expect that's why we're so frequently wrong.

I fully expected to find Grim and all four women waiting for the rest of us, either outside the door of the house or else just inside it. I also expected to find Narayan Singh standing there, for he had ridden on the platform behind the women's carriage, and would naturally get down to open the carriage door for them. I couldn't have guessed wider of the mark. It was a one hundred per cent. miss.

We stepped out into darkness. The other carriage was already disappearing into deeper gloom, and ours proceeded to follow it. There was a porch in such deep shadow that you could hardly see its outlines, but enough dim light came out through the partly opened front door to prove that nobody was standing outside. Somebody standing behind the door opened it wide, and we walked in one by one, Strange leading.

The door clicked softly shut behind us, and it was almost too dark to see, for there was only one lamp in the hall, and that shrouded with black silk; but we could dimly discern three solemn individuals dressed in black from head to foot, who stood in line to receive us. They looked like undertakers.

"Your weapons, please!" said the man in the center in sepulchral tones; and all three held their right hands out.

"Do we get brass checks?" asked Jeremy. The middle man of the three didn't answer, but continued holding out his hand. Meldrum Strange said crustily that he had no weapons.

"Do you mean that we won't be admitted otherwise?" I demanded.

There was still not a word said in reply, but the first and third men each took a threatening step toward Jeremy and me. They obviously meant to search us, and I can't say what I would have done about it, except that I never yet did surrender a weapon to anybody on demand, and old dogs find it difficult to learn new tricks.

But Strange solved the problem for us, by going clear off his head. I guess the nervous strain was too much for a man of his temperament, used to having his own way in the world.

"You swine!" he said; and clenching his right fist he swung with all his strength and weight for the chin of the man in the middle. It was the sort of blow that wins world's championships. Any man caught off-guard would have gone down under it. The fellow in black collapsed like a corpse.

I'm entitled to no credit for what followed. Jeremy did the thinking. I simply followed suit, doing the only thing I could do. Jeremy closed with his man, and I believe hit him with the butt-end of his Colt. The fellow in front of me tried to stop my left fist with the peak of his jaw, and the men who can do that successfully bulk about twice his size.

It was all over in half a second almost noiselessly, for they fell on thick carpet, making no remarks. There was a door on Jeremy's left and he opened it.

"Quick!" he whispered. "Here's an empty room."

You couldn't see a thing, but Jeremy picked up one man, hove him in there, and turned to help me with the second. I had already gathered up Strange's victim. If you've ever watched the U.S. Navy police throwing their captured drunks into a boat in some foreign port you'll realize that an unconscious man can be handled pretty roughly without being seriously hurt; it's only when they struggle that bones get broken.

I tossed number two through the door on top of Jeremy's number one — or so I supposed — and together we picked up the third man. We swung him like a sack and let go. It was only then, as his feet disappeared through the opening, that we realized that all three had fallen, not on to a floor, nor down-stairs, but down a dark hole where a flight of stairs had probably once been.

They made no noise and we didn't stop to investigate. We locked the door and Jeremy pocketed the key.

If you allow two minutes from the time the front door clicked behind us until that other key was in Jeremy's pocket you'll be well on the right side. The next thing Jeremy did was to find the front-door latch, slide it back, and fix it in that position, so that any rescue party would simply have to turn the big brass knob outside and walk in unannounced. But what to do then was too much for even Jeremy to guess, so I said:

"Grim's inside somewhere. We can't leave Grim and Narayan Singh."

There was nothing in that to argue about; but you can suggest as many explanations of what followed as you like without being sure you have given the right one. A friend in the U.S. Secret Service, whom I have known for twenty years, laughed when I told him it couldn't be explained; he said:

"Me boy, that's aisy. Crooks are just crooks. Ivery mother's son has a quirk in him that works wan way. If it weren't for that we'd niver catch the smart wans. They're all alike. They play safe. Be damned, they take more pains playin' safe than a boid takes buildin' a nest. But did you iver see a boid take an inventory wance the nest was built an' the eggs laid? They figure that when precaution's took, it's took. An' that's where we come in. We look for their precautions. It's as plain as the nose on y'r face that those crooks had set three men at the front door 'at they knew they could bet on. An' bet they did. An' bettin's chancy. Chance is scaircely iver on the side of the law, because the law don't dale in chances, but in the long run it's always agin the crook!"

Maybe Clancy put his finger on it — I don't know. The gang upstairs had certainly left the guarding of the entrance hall exclusively to those three men. They were careless when they least could afford to be. We went forward.

There was no furniture in the hall, except two carpets one on top of the other presumably to deaden footfall, and that one dim hanging lantern shrouded in black silk. The stairs turned around to the right in front of us, and we walked up as softly as we could, I leading this time and going slowly.

After making two turns they gave on to a dark landing, also thickly carpeted, and we found ourselves faced by six shut doors, with a window on our left that admitted moonlight through its narrow top pane; the rest was curtained. There was nobody waiting to receive us, but we could hear voices. I cleared my throat loudly; and a wooden shutter moved on the panel of the door immediately in front of us, exposing a small round hole. Light streamed through the hole and was shut off instantly by the head of some one who scrutinized us for about a minute. Then the whole panel moved downward, and his face appeared in the opening, but you couldn't see much of it; the upper half was covered with a black mask; the lower part, that you could see, framed a mean, anemic smile.

"Simon should have brought you upstairs," he complained suspiciously. "Why didn't he?"

Jeremy lied with genius — for I suppose that is genius which gets believed.

"There were three men downstairs," he said. "Two of 'em

went and stood on the porch in the dark. Simon closed the front door and told us to come on up."

"Oh. Well, Simon knows his business. Come in here."

We entered a room about ten by eight that had doors on either hand opening into other rooms. We were in the middle of a suite of apartments. The heat in this small connecting room was stifling, for there was no window and the light came from a huge oil-lamp against which about a hundred moths were busy beating themselves to death.

The man who admitted us had evening clothes on, but over them, in addition to the mask, a black cloak like a pew-opener's that reached his heels, and he seemed to be sweating more than was good for him.

"Where's Grim?" demanded Jeremy.

He didn't answer but, whether intentionally or not, permitted the front of his cloak to open and show a heavy revolver in a holster. Through the door on the left we could hear women's voices — men's through the door on the right; no words were distinguishable. There was no furniture in the room except a carpet, a camp-stool, and the lamp on a bracket on the wall. Our host sat down on the stool between the two side doors, and there seemed to be nothing for us to do but wait and look at him. But waiting isn't Jeremy's favorite amusement.

"Damned uninteresting cage!" he said. "What's in the next one?"

"Wait for your turn!" the man in the mask answered.

"Turn?" said Jeremy. "We're done to a turn! So are you. Let some air in. If you don't, I will!"

"Keep quiet!" said the man in the mask.

"What d'you take us for?" asked Jeremy, purposely raising his voice, and striding forward to open one of the doors. But his purpose was already accomplished. The door on our left opened suddenly and Narayan Singh's face appeared; he smiled, said nothing whatever, and closed the door again at once. Strange looked alarmed, for when Narayan Singh is deliberately trying to look like a hasheesh-maddened fanatic a sight of him would freeze his own mother's marrow-bones. But there wasn't anything reassuring that I could safely say to Strange just then in front of that fellow with a mask.

Jeremy was just about to irritate him further when somebody tapped out a signal on the right-hand door, and with a bad-tempered sneer at us the fellow got off his camp-stool and produced a key from under his cloak. He very nearly unmasked us in the process, for as he made that movement Jeremy and I both felt for our pistols. Luckily he was too intent on fitting the key into the door to notice it.

We went in one by one, passing around a high black screen beyond the door, and found ourselves in a square room furnished with a long mahogany table in the midst, and about a dozen high-backed chairs. There was no other furniture, except for a bench against one wall on which three men were seated.

Facing us at the table as we entered were five men, all in evening clothes. Those on the bench against the wall wore long black cloaks exactly like that of the fellow in the anteroom. Every one of the eight men in the room was masked to the tip of his nose; but the middle one of the five was recognizable from Narayan Singh's account, for he had rolls of fat protruding over his collar, and the end man on our right had a short beard "of the kind that missionaries wear."

We heard the key turn in the lock behind us, which was hardly reassuring, but there were no weapons in evidence, and there was nothing on the table except blotting-paper, pens, ink-pots, and a lot of printed blanks that looked like checks and promissory notes.

"Good evening, Mr. Meldrum Strange! Good evening, gentlemen!" said the man with the fat neck. "Pray be seated."

"Evening!" Strange answered gruffly.

"Where's Grim?" demanded Jeremy.

"Be seated — be seated, gentlemen!"

"Where's Grim?"

"You will learn that presently. Be seated."

We sat down facing the five. There was a door in the middle of the wall behind their backs, and another door on our right, so that we were obviously open to attack from two sides and behind, to say nothing of the three attendants on the bench. There wasn't much to be gained in the circumstances by glancing about the room nervously, so I concentrated my attention on the fat-necked man, reasoning that if there were going to be any violence he would be the one to give the signal. Strange concentrated on him too.

"See here," Strange began, with his right fist set characteristically on the table in front of him. "I made my conditions plain this afternoon. Negotiations are to be between my organization and yours. One of my men, who entered this house ahead of us, is missing. Where is he? He has got to sit here on this side of the table before negotiations can begin!"

"Pardon me, Mr. Meldrum Strange," said the thick-necked man, with that sort of suave inflection that suggests sarcasm without exactly expressing it. "Do you consider yourself in a position to dictate to us?"

"I do! If you think you can deal with me on any but my own conditions, you'll discover your mistake," Strange answered, pulling out a cigar case. "Produce my friend Grim, or there'll be no conference!"

He proceeded to chew the cigar. One of the five pushed over a box of matches. Strange ignored it.

"Well, Mr. Strange," said the thick-necked man, "I may as well tell you first as well as last that your friend Grim has been in here and has been examined. The examination was unsatisfactory — to him, I mean. Your organization will have to get along without him."

"Just exactly what the Hell d'you mean by that?" demanded Strange.

The thick-necked rascal smiled.

"We asked him two questions. The first was, whether he is willing, in the possible event of your rejecting our proposal, to cut your throat in our presence. The second was whether he is willing to commit suicide. He answered both questions in the negative. His answer to the first made it clear to us that he is not to be depended on; his answer to the second proves him to be a man who is blind to his own best interest. Suicide is easy; murder is unfortunately sometimes — well — you know how ill-mannered and rough the underworld can be!"

CHAPTER XI

"Ho!"

"My dear Mr. Strange —"

Meldrum Strange snapped his jaw shut and sat bolt upright. The cigar dropped to the floor; he had bitten off the end of it.

"I'll have no dealings with you whatever until you produce Major Grim!" he said sharply.

"My dear Mr. Strange," the thick-necked man repeated, "you have put yourself entirely in our power. Do let me impress that on your mind! You have no weapons. We have an assortment of them. Your party consists of three. There are three men sitting on that bench. If they should fail, there are plenty more in the next room, and we five are not exactly impotent or without experience. No noise that you might make would do you any good, for the houses to right and left are each more than a hundred yards away, and incidentally they are both empty. So, unless we come to terms —"

"You have my ultimatum!" answered Strange. "Produce Major Grim!"

All five men smiled; and the masked men on the bench moved restlessly, perhaps to call attention to themselves. The man with the thick neck took up the argument again.

"Of course, Mr. Strange, we appreciate that we are dealing with a gentleman of iron nerve and resolution. In fact, we pay you the highest compliment in our power when we invite you to apply for membership in our society. Permit me to elaborate that. Our rule is that applicants for membership must pass through a great number of degrees, entailing severe tests as each higher degree is reached. There is a system of constantly increasing guarantees. We require every member to be so involved in illegal transactions that his liberty and even his life rests on our discretion. Hitherto there have been hardly any exceptions to that rule; but we have decided to make you an exception. You see, Mr. Strange: it is our experience that only men of high character, whose habit is to keep their given word, and at the same time to be ruthless in their dealings, are fit to share the control of our society. We consider you that kind of man."

Strange pulled out another cigar and started to chew it, but made no answer. The thick-necked man continued:

"We have decided after due deliberation that all we shall require from you — without specifying for the moment the financial part; that we will come to later — is an apparent crime. To a man in your peculiar circumstances murder would be exceedingly distasteful and might even result in undermining your nerve. In our profession we find the study of psychology extremely useful. And after all, what courts consider evidence is the principal thing. So, if you and your two friends will carry the bodies of the two men whom you shot in the Pyramid passage, and throw them into the Nile in the presence of witnesses, whom we have ready, we will be satisfied."

"You say we killed two men?" Strange demanded.

"Well, not exactly. You killed one. The other was injured, and if we had taken him to hospital there might have been inconvenient inquiries. The corpses are downstairs. The way to the Nile lies straight down the garden belonging to this house."

"Hell!" exclaimed Jeremy. "I hoped we were in for a real initiation, with red-hot pokers and a black goat! Soon as I'm a member there'll be changes made! I know stacks of ways of making an initiation hum. We'll have it creepy, and —"

The whole executive committee waved aside the interruption.

"Permit me to continue," said the chairman. "Mr. Strange, we may as well outline the whole of our requirements to begin with. You must agree and give the required guarantees, or share the fate of Major Grim. Now, among the guarantees we require that you shall marry Madame Zelmira Poulakis, and settle on her cash or negotiable securities to the amount of a million pounds. She is a charming widow, on whose account you will have no qualms when introducing her as your wife into United States society. At the same time she appreciates and understands our point of view and is sufficiently controlled by us to make her a suitable consort for you. She is waiting close at hand, with witnesses, to sign a marriage contract."

"You lucky old stiff!" laughed Jeremy, nudging Strange in the ribs. Accidentally he nudged the spot that the bullet had touched in the Pyramid passage, and Strange swore explosively.

"For the treasure chest of the Society," the chairman went on, "all that we require from you is half a million pounds. We propose to make further enormous sums with your aid in the United States. An agent of ours in the United States, who has access to the income tax returns, has informed us that your accumulated resources amount to nearly a thousand million dollars. We have no wish to impoverish you. Our plan is that you shall select certain stocks dealt in on the New York Stock Exchange and, after notifying us, accumulate them steadily. We shall buy the same stocks. What is called a bull market will ensue, and we will all unload on the public when you give the signal."

Meldrum Strange began to smile at last, and I think the chairman mistook that for a symptom of complaisance.

"You see," he said, "we are not requiring you to engage in a business that you don't thoroughly understand. This Society likes nothing so well as to see its individual members prosperous — although too much prosperity is not always good for the lower ranks and is seldom permitted for that reason. We like power. We enjoy the power that the secret use of money and influence provides. We keep the power in the right hands. We keep an absolute hold over all our members. Subject to that, you may say we have no use for an indigent or helpless member."

"You've heard my condition," said Strange. "Produce Major Grim before I'll as much as consider your proposal."

The chairman didn't answer, but changed his tone.

"Mr. Strange, permit me to show you the reverse side of this exceedingly attractive medal. Let us suppose that you are unwise enough to reject this offer. What then? Well, in the first place, your two friends will be killed at once. You will see that happen, and for the sake of its effect on you the process will be painful and somewhat prolonged. After that, you will be given your choice between a swift, quite painless death or one even more atrociously disagreeable than theirs that you will have witnessed. For the privilege of dying painlessly, you will have to pay whatever sum we name, signing before witnesses such papers as we shall set before you; and, as it won't make much difference to a dead man how much money he has paid to escape torture, the sum demanded will be — er — well — immodest!

"Let us clearly understand one another, Mr. Strange. This business will be settled in this house this night, one way or the other, and you have no alternative but to join our Society or die. Moreover, you can only become a member on the terms we stipulate."

Undoubtedly psychology did form one of the principal ingredients in that executive committee's method. They had their moves worked out carefully. The chairman brought his speech to an end by rapping on the table with an ebony ruler, and the answer to that was as instant as if the actors in the drama had been drilled for weeks.

We heard the voice of Narayan Singh raised in a babel of Punjabi, pitched high and quarrelsome, behind the door we had entered by. It was followed by a terrific pounding on the door; but as that only made the executive committee smile, none of us was much disturbed by it. Nevertheless, something was going to happen, that was obvious. Something staged in advance.

The voice behind the door was that of a fanatic declaiming. The words seemed a jumble of jabbering nonsense, out of which "kill — kill — kill" in its various tenses emerged in a frequent scream. Then the speech changed to English.

"I tell you I have killed him! Let me show them! They called me a coward! They said I did not dare! They said I loved him! They lied! They lied! Let me through to prove they lied! I will show them the corpse! I will cut the head from the shoulders in their presence! Open that door and let me show them, or I will slay you! Open, I say! Open!"

The pounding on the door resumed more fiercely, to the accompaniment of blasphemous torrents in three languages, such as the half-breeds use in Bombay when the drink is in and they revile both sets of ancestors; only it was worse than I ever heard from a half-breed, for it had more imagination. The chairman leaned over the table and smiled at us.

"That is your Indian friend," he said. "No doubt he looked nice and mild this evening in attendance on Madame Poulakis. We selected him on purpose, because of his known previous loyalty to you. A little hypnotism goes a long way with Indians, but a little drug that we use in such cases goes longer yet! It makes even a white man murdering mad. But you shall see for yourselves."

He made a sign to the men on the bench and one of them walked over to the door, where he tapped a signal. A moment later we heard the key rattling in the lock, and then, knocking down the screen before him like a whirlwind, Narayan Singh strode in with blazing eyes, brandishing his scimitar and dragging Grim by the collar with his left hand.

Grim hung inert and dropped to the floor like a sack when Narayan Singh let go of him. I couldn't detect the slightest sign of breathing, and when I stooped to feel his back — for he lay face-downward — Narayan Singh swore savagely and lunged with his scimitar within two inches of my neck.

You wouldn't have believed he was the same man who had talked with me in Shepheard's Hotel an hour or so before. There was spittle running down his beard. His mouth was all awry with frenzy. His breath came in volcanic gasps, as if the fires of Hell were burning in him, and every muscle in his body seemed to be twitching in unnatural excitement. We three jumped to our feet; there was no sitting down in face of that ghastliness — at least, not for us; the committee seemed to like it.

"Yah!" he yelled, brandishing the scimitar until the air whistled and the blade rang. "I am Hathi the elephant, and I am *musth,* and whom I love I kill! I am the wrath of all the gods! I slay! I am the sword of the Avenger! I work for Yum!"

I don't know what the next amazement of the program would have been. Incredulity fought against the evidence of eyes and ears. There lay my good friend Grim stone dead, so what was the use of recalling what the Sikh had said when sober? He was drunk and drugged now — worse than a blood-crazed wolf. It crossed my mind to shoot him, but Meldrum Strange without meaning to or knowing what had crossed my mind stepped between us.

"You swine!" he thundered, facing the committee. "You dogs! You dirty, cowardly, sneaking, filthy swine! Kill me and be damned to you! That suits me perfectly. Kill me and see what happens! If there's a God, as I believe, the whole foul pack of you will hang!"

"But you see, we're not superstitious," smiled the chairman, veiling savagery under a quiet sneer. "Very well, we shall have to kill you, for you mustn't escape to tell tales about us. We always keep our promises. Guards!"

The three men rose together from the bench and started for us — in no hurry — they seemed very sure of themselves.

Jeremy and I drew our pistols. Instantly one of then shouted for help; but he only got one word out, for I drilled him clean and he dropped. The crack of my repeating pistol turned chaos loose.

Grim came suddenly to life almost between my legs — Narayan Singh turned sane and sober. Grim rushed the table on all fours — upturned it on the committee of five — and shoved me with all his might, saying nothing. Jeremy and Narayan Singh took either end of it, and shoved too, upsetting all five chairs. I heard Narayan Singh laugh, and the pistols going like a machine-gun as the scrambling committee tried to shoot through the table-top, or under, or around it — loosing off like crazy men as they struggled among the chairs, hoping to kill with a chance shot, or summon help, or both.

But I couldn't stop to help or look, I had my hands full. One of the three guards rushed for the right-hand door and tugged at it, shouting to some one on the other side, and the third man opened fire on me at a distance of twelve feet. I shot him, but too low, for he lay on the floor and continued to blaze away at me. He got me in two places, and I felt the bone of my left forearm go numb. Meanwhile, the third man had dragged the door open; and a dozen men, all masked, came running in with knives and pistols. It looked like our good-by, whatever else it might be.

I STEPPED in front of Meldrum Strange, who was out of breath from shoving at the table, and managed to drop three men, one after another, as they entered; a fourth fell over the first three, and that ended my present usefulness, for my pistol was empty, and with my left arm out of action I couldn't reload it, although I had a spare clip in my vest pocket. I shouted to Jeremy, who cut loose in my stead, and the room began to look like a shambles. Meldrum Strange reloaded my pistol, fumbling with excited fingers, and the enemy beat a retreat to consider a new method of attack, slamming shut the door they had entered by, and smashing a panel in order to shoot through it from cover.

But everything happened at once. None of us was clear afterward as to the exact sequence of events. I balked the hole-in-the-door game by picking up the bench the three men had sat on throughout the interview and upending it against the door — a temporary stop-gap, but a good one while it lasted. Strange came and added his weight to mine. They smashed a second panel, but we lifted up the bench and held it crosswise. It seemed there was a narrow passage outside that prevented them from bringing all their weight to bear against the door, and we two held it shut for I dare say two minutes.

Meanwhile Grim and Narayan Singh, both without firearms — for the men downstairs had deprived Grim of his pistol at the front door — were beginning to have the worst of it. They had the table shoved all the way back against the third door with its legs against the wall; and in the space so left, crouching among upset chairs, the committee of five were about impregnable. Narayan Singh was alert with his scimitar to swipe at the first hand or head that showed, and Jeremy stood back with pistol ready, but it was likely to be only a matter of seconds before a volley of shots should end that situation.

Then two things began to happen simultaneously. Men began trying to burst open the door behind the table, but the table, committee, and chairs added to the weight of Grim and Narayan Singh prevented that for the moment, until it dawned on the five that they only had to set their legs against the wall and shove in order to release the door and admit their friends.

Just as they commenced doing that, the door by which we had entered the room burst open and five screaming women struggled in, forcing along in front of them the masked man who had admitted us. He was trying to help four of them restrain Zelmira Poulakis, who was using a long thing like a hat-pin to some purpose. And just as the struggling potpourri of women forced him backward into the room the man drew his revolver and aimed at Zelmira's head point blank. Jeremy shot him promptly, drilling a hole exactly through his temples.

That staggered the four women for a moment — three of them were the same who had attended our dinner-party —

and Zelmira shook herself partly free of them. She was a wild sight with her bronze hair down and her clothes ripped nearly off her, bleeding where the other women had torn her with their finger-nails, but beautiful in spite of it — or maybe because of it, for there was courage there, as well as frenzy; furious action in place of masked intrigue.

"Kill those five — the committee of five!" she screamed. "Kill those monsters! Are you men! Kill those devils before you die!"

Strange and I could no longer hold that door we had propped the bench against. They burst it off its hinges and we sprang back to the center of the room. I shot the first two men who entered, Jeremy shot another, but the rest rushed, and when my pistol was empty a second time three of them closed with me. I had only one hand to fight with. Three more of them pounced on Strange, and one man, standing in the door, fired on Zelmira, but missed her and killed one of the other women.

"Kill those five! Oh, kill them!" Zelmira Poulakis screamed. "Never mind the others! Do a good deed! Kill those five monsters!"

Then the door behind the table burst inward and half a dozen men stepped forward cautiously between the upset chairs and the scrambling committee. The committee got to their knees to shoot over the table-edge and it looked as if the end had come.

"There they are! Kill them!" Zelmira screamed.

I saw them killed. I was down under three men, struggling to break the neck of one, whose head was in chancery under my right arm. A second lay still on top of me, for Jeremy had brained him with the butt-end of his pistol, and the third was trying to hold my legs, which is no job for a weakling. I turned my head to see what was happening to Strange, whom Jeremy was doing his best to preserve alive until the last possible second, when that scimitar flashed across my line of vision — flashed like Summer lightning under the hanging lamp.

Gosh! But I never saw the like of it — I, who have seen the

sword-dance under Sikaram when the rival clans were showing off before the women! I've seen a shark, too, taking fish — left-right, left-right, and away again; and more than once I've seen a lion spring between the watch-fires, make his kill, and escape. But never, on all the continents, have I seen action that could hold a candle to that sword-work of Narayan Singh's.

He slew those five committee-men in five strokes so swift that they resembled one, and then went blazing, berserker mad in mid-room, swinging, swiping, lunging, shouting "Ho!" as his blade struck home, and driving the astonished foe in front of him as a bull clears men out of a field.

Some of them fired, but fired and ran too quickly for straight aim, most of them facing him, but crowding backward in one another's way; and in thirty seconds more the thing was over. Kennedy stood in the door of the anteroom in evening dress, smiling, holding a loaded pistol behind his back.

"That will do now," he said quietly. His voice had that peculiar penetrating quality that I had noticed in the hotel when he first came forward to meet me.

And it did do, for behind him, and through both the other doors, his hand-picked corps of officers came surging in; and one of the most peculiar things in this cantankerous old world is the resemblance between a sudden fight and an explosion. When it's over, it's over — done with — nothing left of it but wreckage and the acrid smell of powder.

Kennedy's arrangements had been neat, and they worked in the nick of time, which of course is a sign of genius; but as Grim argued afterward, over a whisky and soda with a man whose name must not appear, if he hadn't been so particularly careful to catch all the small fry by first surrounding the house and then having his posse enter from every side at once, he might have taken those five principals alive; and that in turn might have led to the capture of worse rascals higher up.

But, as Kennedy suggested, it wasn't a bad night's work for all that. There were ambulances ready, and we had twenty-eight living prisoners including women to stow in them, all of whom had seen the committee-men killed and, no longer having them to fear, were anxious to tell all they knew.

Some of the officers drove away with the prisoners, to see them safely under lock and key, and the rest of us, with Zelmira Poulakis, foregathered in another room to patch up wounds and compare notes.

CHAPTER XII

"I but acted as other men would act!"

ZELMIRA POULAKIS HAD the floor first, when old Narendra Nath had finished putting strips of plaster on her scratches. We found the old man cowering in another room, making magic under cover of a purple cloak.

"I don't care what happens now," she said. "I have been a criminal ever since I was married; first because Poulakis taught me, and it seemed good fun; later on because I was compelled. I hoped this forced marriage to Mr. Meldrum Strange might prove a way of escape for me. I didn't believe he would marry me, and yet I half-hoped he would, because there was no other hope in sight.

"And then this Indian, Narayan Singh, said that if Major Grim and his friends had anything to do with Meldrum Strange, then Meldrum Strange was *'pakka,'* as he called it, and he offered to wager his right hand against my slipper that if he could only talk with any of the *sahibs* there would be no doubt of the outcome. So it was agreed that when we reached the hotel this evening he should seize his opportunity."

"She speaks truth," said Narayan Singh. "But I have told my end of the tale already to Ramsden *sahib.* Let Jimgrim tell the rest. Those women had orders to bring Jimgrim in their carriage, and I had orders to slay him; but old Narendra Nath, who brought the order to me, knowing well by that time that his magic took no effect on me, bade me not slay.

" 'I am an old man,' said he, 'and I dare not wholly disobey these men; but I have seen a vision, and the stars are favorable. So I say; 'slay not, but make believe to fall in with the plan.'

"And so I did as he said, being minded to do so in any case, whether he so advised or not. And when we reached this house, and the men at the door disarmed Jimgrim, I seized him from behind, whispering two words in his ear; and I dragged him upstairs into a room beside that in which the women waited. There he and I held a conference, and later I did as Jimgrim bade me."

"Then it wasn't true," I asked, "that Grim was taken before the committee and examined ahead of us?"

"No, not a word of truth in that," Grim answered. "Narayan Singh gave me the general layout; and I knew that Kennedy had most of the facts from Ramsden, so it was a reasonable gamble, as well as our only chance, that Kennedy would act swiftly. I've worked under Kennedy, and know his method fairly well; I figured he'd surround the house and rush it. So the one important thing to do was to gain time. Narayan Singh had orders to produce me — dead — at a given signal. They thought he was hypnotized and were sure he'd obey. So I had him drag me into the anteroom, and he looked so wild that the fellow in there didn't dare examine me to see whether I was properly dead. But the credit for the whole business belongs to Narayan Singh. My share in it was —"

"Nay, nay, *sahib!*" the Sikh answered. "I but acted as any other man would act. I take no credit. I did no more than to scout a little, and convey my information to the proper quarter. Yet, if there is any little merit in what I did — if *burra sahib* Kennedy considers that the *sirkar* is beholden to me — then, there is a favor I might ask, if permission were granted."

"What is it?" demanded Kennedy. "I can't grant requests, you know. I can only recommend that they be granted."

"The lady Zelmira, *sahib* — what is to become of her? I swore to serve her to the end of this affair. I beg, then, that she be not thrown in jail. That is surely a little thing; will the *sahib* grant it?"

Kennedy laughed. Everybody laughed, except Zelmira Poulakis and Narayan Singh. The Sikh looked offended, and she miserable.

"I suppose it must be amusing, since you all find it so," she said, holding her chin up bravely. "But it does not seem funny to me. What do you intend to do with me? May I go home first and get some things?"

"I humbly beg your pardon," Kennedy answered. "We were laughing at our friend Narayan Singh's naïveté, not at your predicament. I don't know, Madame, what is to be done with you. My authority is limited. But if you should offer to turn State's Evidence —"

"Which I do!" she interrupted.

"— and should undertake to help the Administration in every way possible to bring the members of this gang to their deserts —"

"Which I certainly will!" she assured him.

"— then I would take upon myself the responsibility of requesting you to return to your own home, where, if you will stay indoors and keep quiet, you will be subjected for the present to no other inconvenience than a trustworthy guard, who will protect you from gang-vengeance. If your evidence should be accepted by the State, you would afterward be set entirely free."

THE END

LaVergne, TN USA
30 December 2009
168531LV00003B/221/A